SNOWDROPS

SNOWDROPS

A. D. MILLER

HarperCollins Publishers Ltd

Published by HarperCollins Publishers Ltd

First published in Great Britain in 2010 by Atlantic Books, an
imprint of Atlantic Books Ltd.

First Canadian edition

HarperCollins Publishers Ltd
2 Bloor Street East, 20th Floor
Toronto, Ontario, Canada
M4W 1A8

www.harpercollins.ca

Library and Archives Canada Cataloguing in Publication information
is available upon request

ISBN 978-1-55468-783-1

Printed and bound in the United States
HC 9 8 7 6 5 4 3 2 1

Snowdrop. 1. An early-flowering bulbous plant, having a white pendent flower. **2.** *Moscow slang.* A corpse that lies buried or hidden in the winter snows, emerging only in the thaw.

For Arkady, Becky, Guy, Mark and
especially Emma.

I smelled it before I saw it.

There was a crowd of people standing around on the pavement and in the road, most of them policemen, some talking on mobile phones, some smoking, some looking, some looking away. From the way I came, they were blocking my view, and at first I thought that with all the uniforms it must be a traffic accident or maybe an immigration bust. Then I caught the smell. It was a smell like the kind you come home to if you forget to put your rubbish out before you go on holiday – ripe but acidic, strong enough to block out the normal summer aromas of beer and revolution. It was the smell that had given it away.

From about ten metres away, I saw the foot. Just one, as if its owner was stepping very slowly out of a limousine. I can still see the foot now. It was wearing a cheap black slip-on shoe, and above the shoe there was a stretch of grey sock, then a glimpse of greenish flesh.

The cold had kept it fresh, they told me. They didn't know how long it had been there. Maybe all winter, one of the policemen speculated. They'd used a hammer, he said, or possibly a brick. Not a good job, he said. He asked me if I wanted to see the rest of it. I said no, thank you. I'd already seen and learned more than I needed to during that last winter.

You're always saying that I never talk about my time in Moscow or about why I left. You're right, I've always made excuses, and soon you'll understand why. But you've gone on asking me, and for some reason lately I keep thinking about it – I can't stop myself. Perhaps it's because we're only three months away from 'the big day', and that somehow seems a sort of reckoning. I feel like I need to tell someone about Russia, even if it hurts. Also that probably you should know, since we're going to make these promises to each other, and maybe even keep them. I think you have a right to know all of it. I thought it would be easier if I wrote it down. You won't have to make an effort to put a brave face on things, and I won't have to watch you.

So here is what I've written. You wanted to know how it ended. Well, that was almost the end, that afternoon with the foot. But the end really began the year before, in September, in the Metro.

When I told Steve Walsh about the foot, by the way, he said, 'Snowdrop. Your friend is a snowdrop.' That's what the Russians call them, he told me – the bodies that float up into the light in the thaw. Drunks, most of them, and homeless people who just give up and lie down into the whiteness, and murder victims hidden in the drifts by their killers.

Snowdrops: the badness that is already there, always there and very close, but which you somehow manage not to see. The sins the winter hides, sometimes for ever.

ONE

I can at least be sure of her name. It was Maria Kovalenko, Masha to her friends. She was standing on the station platform at Ploshchad Revolyutsii, Revolution Square, when I first caught sight of her. I could see her face for about five seconds before she took out a little make-up mirror and held it in front of her. With her other hand she put on a pair of sunglasses that I remember thinking she might have just bought from a kiosk in an underpass somewhere. She was leaning against a pillar, up at the end of the platform where the civilian statues are – athletes, engineers, bosomy female farmhands and mothers holding muscular babies. I looked at her for longer than I should have.

There's a moment at Ploshchad Revolyutsii, a visual effect

that happens when you're transferring to the green line from that platform with the statues. You find yourself crossing the Metro tracks on a little elevated walkway, and on one side you can see a flotilla of disc-shaped chandeliers, stretching along the platform and away into the darkness that the trains come out of. On the other side you see other people making the same journey, only on a parallel walkway, close but separate. When I looked to the right that day I saw the girl with the sunglasses heading the same way.

I got on the train for the one-stop ride to Pushkinskaya. I stood beneath the yellow panelling and the ancient strip lighting that made me feel, every time I took the Metro, as if I was an extra in some paranoid Donald Sutherland film from the seventies. At Pushkinskaya I went up the escalator with its phallic lamps, held open the heavy glass Metro doors for the person behind me like I always used to, and made my way into the maze of low-slung underground passages beneath Pushkin Square. Then she screamed.

She was about five metres behind me, and as well as screaming she was wrestling against a thin man with a ponytail who was trying to steal her handbag (an ostentatiously fake Burberry). She was screaming for help, and the friend who had appeared alongside her – Katya, it turned out – was just screaming. To begin with I only watched, but the man drew back his fist like he was about to punch her, and I heard someone shouting from behind me as if they were going to do something about it. I stepped forward and pulled the thin man back by his collar.

He gave up on the bag and swung his elbows at me, but they didn't reach. I let go and he lost his balance and fell. It was all over quickly and I didn't get a good enough look at him. He was young, maybe four inches shorter than me, and seemed embarrassed. He stabbed out a foot, catching me painlessly on the shin, and scrambled to his feet and ran away, down the underpass and up the stairs at the far end that led to Tverskaya – the Oxford Street of Moscow, only with lawless parking, which slopes down from Pushkin Square to Red Square. There were two policemen near the bottom of the steps, but they were too busy smoking and looking for immigrants to harass to pay the mugger any attention.

'*Spasibo*,' said Masha. (Thank you.) She took off the sunglasses.

She was wearing tight tight jeans tucked into knee-high brown leather boots, and a white blouse with one more button undone than there needed to be. Over the blouse she had one of those funny Brezhnev-era autumn coats that Russian women without much money often wear. If you look at them closely they seem to be made out of carpet or beach towel with a cat-fur collar, but from a distance they make the girl in the coat look like the honey-trap in a Cold War thriller. She had a straight bony nose, pale skin and long tawny hair, and with a bit more luck she might have been sitting beneath the gold-leaf ceiling in some hyper-priced restaurant called the Ducal Palace or the Hunting Lodge, eating black caviar and smiling indulgently at a nickel magnate or well-connected oil trader. Perhaps that's where she is now, though somehow I doubt it.

'*Oi, spasibo*,' said her friend, clasping the fingers of my right hand. Her hand was warm and light. I reckoned the sunglasses girl was in her early twenties, twenty-three maybe, but the friend seemed younger, nineteen or possibly even less. She was wearing white boots, a pink fake-leather miniskirt and a matching jacket. She had a little upturned nose and straight blond hair, and one of those frankly inviting Russian-girl grins, the ones that come with full-on eye contact. It was a smile like the smile of the baby Jesus we once saw – do you remember? – in that church in the village down the coast from Rimini: the old, wise smile on the young face, a smile that said, *I know who you are, I know what you want, I was born knowing this.*

'*Nichevo*,' I said. (It was nothing.) And again in Russian I added, 'Is everything okay?'

'*Vso normalno*,' said the sunglasses girl. (Everything is normal.)

'*Kharasho*,' I said. (Good.)

We smiled at each other. My glasses had steamed up in the cloying year-round warmth of the Metro. One of the CD kiosks in the passageway was playing folk music, I remember, the lyrics choked out by one of those drunken Russian chanteurs who sound like they must have started smoking in the womb.

In a parallel universe, in another life, that's the end of the story. We say goodbye, I go home that afternoon and back to my lawyering the next day. Maybe in that life I'm still there, still in Moscow, maybe I found another job and stayed, never came home and never met you. The girls go on to whoever and whatever it would have been if it hadn't been me. But I was flushed with that feeling you get when a risky thing goes well, and the high of having done something good. A noble deed in a ruthless place. I was a small-time hero, they'd let me be one, and I was grateful.

The younger one carried on smiling, but the older one was just looking. She was taller than her friend, five nine or ten, and in her heels her green eyes were level with mine. They are lovely eyes. Someone had to say something, and she said, in English, 'Where are you from?'

I said, 'I'm from London.' I'm not from London originally, as you know, but it's close enough. In Russian I asked, 'And where are you from?'

'Now we live here in Moscow,' she said. I was used to this language game by then. The Russian girls always said they wanted to practise their English. But sometimes they also wanted to make you feel that you were in charge, in their country but safe in your own language.

There was another smiling pause.

'*Tak, spasibo*,' said the friend. (So, thank you.)

None of us moved. Then Masha said, 'To where are you going?'

'Home,' I said. 'Where are you going?'

'We are only walking.'

'*Poguliaem*,' I said. (Let's walk.)

And we did.

* * *

It was the middle of September. It's the time of year Russians call 'grandma's summer' – a bittersweet lick of velvety warmth that used to arrive after the peasant women had brought in their harvests, and now in Moscow means last-gasp outdoor drinking in the squares and around the Bulvar (the lovely old road around the Kremlin that has stretches of park between the lanes, with lawns, benches and statues of famous writers and forgotten revolutionaries). It's the nicest time to visit, though I'm not certain we ever will. The stalls outside the

Metro stations were laying out their fake-fur Chinese gloves for the coming winter, but there were still long lines of tourists waiting to file through Lenin's freak-show tomb in Red Square. In the hot afternoons half the women in the city were still wearing almost nothing.

We came up the smooth narrow steps from the underground passages beneath the square, arriving outside the Armenian supermarket. We crossed the gridlocked lanes of traffic to the broad pavement in the middle of the Bulvar. There was only one cloud in the sky, plus a fluffy plume of smoke flying up from a factory or inner-city power plant, just visible against the early evening blue. It was beautiful. The air smelled of cheap petrol, grilled meat and lust.

The older one asked, in English, 'What is your job in Moscow, if it is not secret?'

'I am a lawyer,' I said in Russian.

They spoke to each other very quickly, too fast and low for me to understand.

The younger one said, 'For how much years you have been in Moscow?'

'Four years,' I said. 'Nearly four years.'

'Are you liking it?' said the sunglasses girl. 'Are you liking our Moscow?'

I said that I liked it very much, which is what I thought she'd

11

want to hear. Most of them had a sort of automatic national pride, I'd discovered, even if all they wanted for themselves was to get the hell out of there and head for Los Angeles or the Côte d'Azur.

'And what do you do?' I asked her in Russian.

'I am working in shop. For mobile phones.'

'Where is your shop?'

'Across river,' she said. 'Close to Tretyakov Gallery.' After a few silent paces she added, 'You speak beautiful Russian.'

She exaggerated. I spoke better Russian than most of the carpet-bagging bankers and mountebank consultants in the city – the pseudo-posh Englishmen, strong-toothed Americans and misleading Scandinavians the black-gold rush had brought to Moscow, who mostly managed to shuttle between their offices, gated apartments, expense-account brothels, upscale restaurants and the airport on twenty-odd words. I was on my way to being fluent, but my accent still gave me away halfway through my first syllable. Masha and Katya must have clocked me as a foreigner even before I opened my mouth. I suppose I was easy to spot. It was a Sunday, and I was on my way home from some awkward expat get-together in a lonely accountant's flat. I was wearing new-ish jeans and suede boots, I remember, and a dark V-neck sweater with a Marks & Spencer's shirt underneath. People didn't dress like that in Moscow. Anybody with money went in for film-star shirts and Italian shoes, and everybody without money, which was most people, wore contraband army surplus, or cheap Belarussian boots and bleak trousers.

Masha, on the other hand, was authentically beautiful in English, even if her grammar was shaky. Some Russian women shoot up into a sort of over-elocutioned squeak when they speak English, but she had a voice that dropped down, almost to a growl, hungrily rolling her Rs. Her voice sounded like it had been through an all-night party. Or a war.

We were walking towards the beer tents that go up for the summer on the first warm day in May, when the whole city takes to the streets and anything can happen, and are folded up again in October when grandma's summer is over.

'Tell me, please,' said the younger one. 'My friend said me that in England you have two...'

She broke off to confer with her companion in Russian. I heard 'hot', 'cold', 'water'.

'What is it called,' the older one said, 'where water comes? In bathroom?'

'Taps.'

'Yes, taps,' the younger one went on. 'My friend said me that in England there is two taps. So hot water sometimes is burning her hand.'

'*Da, eta pravda,*' I said. (Yes, it's true.) We were on a path in the middle of the Bulvar, near some seesaws and wobbly slides. A fat babushka was selling apples.

'And is it true,' she said, 'that in London is always big fog?'

'*Nyet,*' I said. 'A hundred years ago, yes, but not any more.'

She looked down at the ground. Masha, the sunglasses girl, smiled. When I think back on what I liked about her that first afternoon, apart from the long firm gazelle body, and the voice, and her eyes, it was the irony. She had an air that suggested she already knew how it would end, and almost wanted me to know that too. Maybe this is just how it seems to me now, but in a way I think she was already apologizing. I think that for her, people and their actions were somehow separate – as if you could just bury whatever you did and forget about it, as if your past belonged to someone else.

We reached the junction with my street. I had that drunk feeling that, before you, I always used to get in the company of premier-league women – half nervous, half rash, like I was acting, like I was living in someone else's life and had to make the most of it while I could.

I gestured and said, 'I live over here.' Then I heard myself say, 'Would you like to come up for some tea?'

You'll think it sounds ridiculous, I know, me trying it on like that. But only a couple of years before, when foreigners

were still considered exotic in Moscow and a lawyer was someone with a salary worth saying yes to, it might have worked. It
had worked.

She said no.

'But if it is interesting for you to call us,' she said, 'you may.'
She looked at her friend, who took a pen from the pocket above
her left breast and wrote a phone number on the back of a trolley-bus ticket. She held it out to me, and I took it.

'My name is Masha,' she said. 'This is Katya. She is my sister.'

'I'm Nick,' I said.

Katya leaned against me in her pink skirt and kissed me on
the cheek. She smiled the other smile that they have, the Asiatic
smile that means nothing. They walked away down the Bulvar,
and I watched them for longer than I should have.

* * *

The Bulvar was full of boozers and sleepers and kissers. Gangs
of teenagers clustered around squatting guitarists. It was still
warm enough for all the windows of the restaurant on the corner of my street to be thrown open, ventilating the minigarch
and mid-range hooker crowd that used to congregate there
in the summer. I had to walk in the road to avoid the long,
unimaginative sequence of black Mercedes and Hummers that
had overrun the pavements around it. I turned into my street

and walked along the side of the mustard-coloured church on the way to my flat.

I guess it might actually have been another day – maybe the image just seems to belong with the meeting on the Metro, so I remember them together – but in my mind it was the same evening that I first noticed the old Zhiguli. It was on my side of the street, sandwiched between two BMWs like a ghost of Russia past, or the answer to a simple odd-one-out puzzle. It was shaped like a child's drawing of a car: a box on wheels, with another box on top in which the child might add a stick-man driver and his steering wheel, and silly round headlights on which, if he was feeling exuberant, the child would circle pupils to make them look like eyes. It was the sort of car that most of the men in Moscow had once spent half their lives waiting to buy, or so they were always telling you, saving and coveting and putting their names on waiting lists to get one, only to find – after the wall came down, they got America on TV and their better-connected compatriots got late-model imports – that even their dreams had been shabby. It was hard to be sure, but this one had probably once been a sort of rusty orange colour. It had mud and oil up its flanks, like a tank might after a battle – a dark crust that, if you were frank with yourself, you knew was how your insides looked after a few years in Moscow, and maybe your soul too.

The pavement on the way to my entrance had been left to dissolve into the road in the way that Russian pavements tend to. I walked past the churchyard and the Zhiguli to my building, punched in my code on the intercom and went inside.

I lived in one of the Moscow apartment blocks that were built as grand houses by doomed well-to-do merchants, just before the revolution. Like the city itself, it had been slapped about so much that it had come to look like several different buildings mashed together. An ugly lift had been fixed on to the outside and a fifth storey added to the top, but it had kept the original swirling ironwork of its staircase. Most of the front doors to the individual apartments were made of axe-resistant steel, but had been prettified with a sort of leather padding – a fashion that sometimes made it feel as though the whole of upscale Moscow was a low-security asylum. On the third floor the smell of cat litter and the screech of a nervous-breakdown Russian symphony emerged from my neighbour Oleg Niko-laevich's place. On the fourth I turned the three locks on my padded door and went inside. I went into the kitchen, sat at my little bachelor's table and took the trolley-bus ticket with Masha's phone number on it out of my wallet.

In England, before you, I'd only ever had one thing with a woman that you might seriously call a relationship. You know about her, I think – Natalie. We met at college, though until someone's drunken birthday party somewhere in Shoreditch we hadn't thought of each other as contenders. I don't think either of us had the energy to end it once it had started, and six or seven months later she moved into my old flat without me really agreeing or disagreeing. I wasn't exactly relieved when she moved out again, saying that she needed to think and wanted me to think too, but I wasn't devastated either. We'd lost touch even before I went to Moscow.

There had been a few Russian girls who'd seemed to be on their way to being proper girlfriends, but none of them lasted more than a summer. One became frustrated that I didn't have and wouldn't get the things she wanted and expected: a car, a driver to go with the car, one of those silly little dogs they drag around the designer shops in the cobbled alleys near the Kremlin. There was another one, Dasha I think her name was, who after the third time she stayed over began hiding things in the wardrobe and in the little cabinet above my bathroom sink: a scarf, an empty bottle of perfume, notes that said 'I love you too' in Russian. I asked Steve Walsh about it (you remember Steve, the lechy foreign correspondent – you came along when I met up with him in Soho once and didn't like him). He told me that she was marking her territory, letting anybody else I brought home know that someone else had got there first. By that September you had to be careful who you hooked up with in Moscow – because of AIDS, but also because foreign men were going to clubs, meeting girls, leaving their drinks on the table when they went to take a piss, then waking up without their wallets in the backs of taxis they didn't remember getting in to, or face down in puddles, or once or twice, probably when they got the dose wrong, not waking up at all.

I'd never found what people like my brother had, what my sister thought she had until she didn't, what you and me are signing up for now: the contract, the settlement, the same body only and always – and, in return for all that, the back-up, the pet names and the head-stroking in the night when you feel like crying. I'd always thought I didn't want it, not ever, to tell you the truth, that I could be one of the people who are happier without. I think maybe my parents had put me off the whole thing – starting out too young, banging out the kids without really thinking about it, forgetting whatever it was they liked about each other in the first place. By then it seemed to me my mum and dad were just sitting it out, two old dogs tied to the same kennel but too tired to fight any more. At home they watched television all the time so they didn't have to talk to each other. I'm sure that, on the rare occasions they went out for a meal, they were one of those painful couples you sometimes see chewing together in silence.

But when I met Masha that day in September, somehow I

thought she might be it, 'the one' I hadn't been looking for. The wild chance of it seemed wonderful. Yes it was a physical thing, but not only. Maybe it was just the right time, but straight away I thought I could see her hair falling down the back of a towelling dressing gown as she made the coffee, picture her with her head resting asleep against me on a plane. If I was being blunt with you, I guess I might almost call it 'falling in love'.

The smell of poplar trees crept in through the open windows of my kitchen, along with the sound of sirens and breaking glass. Some of me wanted her to be my future, and some other me wanted to do what I should have done, and throw the ticket with the phone number out of the kitchen window and into the pink and promising evening air.

| TWO

I rang her the next day. In Russia they don't go in so much for the phoney self-restraint, the sham waiting and feints, the whole dating war-game that you and I played in London – and anyway, I'm afraid I couldn't stop myself. I went through to her voicemail and left her my mobile number and my number at the office.

I heard nothing for about three weeks and almost managed to stop thinking about her. Almost. It helped that I was busy at work, like all the western lawyers in Moscow then. Cash was gushing out of the ground in Siberia, and at the same time another flood of money was rolling in. A new breed of Russian conglomerates were frantically dismembering each other, and foreign banks were lending them the billions they needed to make their acquisitions. The bankers and the Russian businessmen came to our office to agree their terms: the bankers in their double-cuff shirts and whitened smiles, the thick-necked ex-KGB oil men in their tight suits, and us, doing the paperwork on the loans and taking our little cut. The office was in a crenellated beige tower on Paveletskaya Square, a building that hadn't quite achieved the air of sleek wealth that its architect had been shooting for, but was nevertheless the air-conditioned daytime home of half the expats in Moscow. On the other side of the square was Paveletsky train station, the domain of drunks and wrecks and glue-sniffing children, poor hopeless bastards who had fallen off the Russian tightrope. The station and the tower stared at each other across the square like mismatched armies before a battle.

There was a clever new secretary at work called Olga, who wore figure-hugging trouser suits and came, I think, from Tatarstan, and who I'm sure is by now running some pipe-importing or lipstick-distribution company, living the new Russian dream. She had deep brown eyes and sensational cheekbones, and we had some nice running banter about how I was going to show her London, and what was she going to show me?

Then towards the middle of October Masha called, and in her growly voice asked me whether I wanted to have dinner with her and Katya.

'Good morning, Nicholas,' she said. 'This is Masha.'

She clearly didn't think she needed to say which Masha, and she was right. I felt my neck flush.

'Hello, Masha, how are you?'

'I am good thank you, Nicholas. Tell me, please, what do you do this evening?'

They're funny, don't you think, those first phone calls, when you talk to the new person who's been living in your head, though you don't really know them yet at all? Those awkward moments that could be a turning point in your life, that could be everything, or could be nothing.

'Nothing,' I said.

'We are inviting you for dinner. Do you know one restaurant that is called Mechta Vostoka?'

'Dream of the East'. I did. It was one of the kitsch Caucasian places that float on big moored platforms in the river opposite Gorky Park – the kind of restaurant proposition that you would turn up your nose at in London, but which in Moscow means summer walks along the embankment, deep red Caucasian wine, other people's nostalgia for sunny Soviet holidays, stupid dancing and freedom. She said they'd booked a table for eight thirty.

* * *

It was the same day, the same afternoon, this time I'm sure it was, that I first met the Cossack. He appeared in our office on the ninth floor of the tower at Paveletskaya, smirking.

We'd been instructed to act for a consortium of western banks on a five-hundred-million-dollar loan, to be paid out in three instalments and repaid at a fat rate of interest. The borrower was a joint venture involving a logistics firm we'd never heard of and Narodneft. (Maybe you remember reading about Narodneft: it's the giant state energy company, which had swallowed the assets the Kremlin strong-armed from the oligarchs using bogus lawsuits and made-up tax demands.) Together they were proposing to construct a floating oil terminal somewhere up in the Barents Sea – I didn't pay too much attention to the geography, to be honest, at least not until I finally went up there. Their plan was to convert a huge Soviet tanker ship to sit stationary in the ocean, with a pipeline from the shore to feed it the oil.

Narodneft was getting ready to list a chunk of its shares in New York and needed its books to look healthy. So, to keep the liabilities for the project off the balance sheet, the management had found a partner and set up a separate company to run it. The project company was registered in the British Virgin Islands. The front man was the Cossack.

The truth is, I liked the Cossack, at least to start with, and I think in a way, in his way, he liked me. Something about him was endearing – the unabashed hedonism, maybe, or the blasé thuggery. It might be better to say I envied him. He was a little man vertically, five feet six or thereabouts, half a foot shorter than me, with a boy-band fringe, a ten-thousand-dollar suit and a murderer's smile. He was equal parts twinkle and menace. He had nothing with him when he slid out of the lift – no briefcase, no papers, no lawyers – except a tank-shaped bodyguard with a shaven turret-shaped head.

I'd drawn up a mandate letter, a sort of preliminary contract, which the Cossack needed to countersign on behalf of his joint venture. We'd faxed a copy to his lawyers a couple of days before: the lead bank undertook to get the money together, roping in a few other banks to spread the risk, while the Cossack promised not to borrow it from anyone else. We led him to the glass-walled meeting room in the corner of our open-plan office. We were me, my boss Paolo, and Sergei Borisovich, one of the keen young Russians in our corporate department. Paolo was well into his forties, but he was still lean and suave in the way that middle-aged Italian men can be, with a picturesque burst of white hair on one side of his head and a wife he avoided as much as possible. He had woken up one morning in the early nineties in his comfortable Milanese bed, picked up the whiff of money wafting in from the east, followed it, and stayed too long. Sergei Borisovich was short, with a face like a perplexed potato. He had finished learning his English on an exchange programme in North Carolina but he had started with MTV, and his favourite word was still 'extreme'.

We passed the document to the Cossack. He turned the first page, turned it back again, pushed the file away, sat back in his chair and puffed out his cheeks. He looked around as if he was waiting for something else to happen – a strip show, maybe, or a stabbing. The blue and gold onion domes of the Novospassky Monastery winked at us through the ninth-floor window from across the Moscow River. And then he started making jokes.

The Cossack had one of those senses of humour that are really a kind of warfare. Laughing at his jokes made you feel guilty, not laughing at them made you feel endangered. His personal enquiries always felt like a prelude to blackmail.

He told us he was a Cossack, from Stavropol, I think it was, or somewhere down there in the southern badlands. Did we know what Cossacks were? It was their historical mission, he explained, to keep the 'blacks' quiet down in the armpit of Russia. Why didn't we come up north to the site of the oil terminal, his new posting, to see him? He would introduce us all to Cossack hospitality.

'Maybe one day,' Paolo replied. I said I had a wife in Moscow who didn't like me going away. That's how I know it was definitely the same day as my dinner with Masha and Katya: because I remember those words, as I said them, feeling like only three-quarters of a lie, only a temporary lie, perhaps.

'Well,' the Cossack said in Russian, 'you can have two wives – one in Moscow and one in the Arctic.'

He smoked a cigarette, baring his teeth. Then he signed the mandate letter without looking at it, belched and grinned. We saw him and his minder to the lift. As he said goodbye he was abruptly sombre: 'Guys,' he said as he shook our hands, 'this is special. Russia is grateful to you.'

'Lipstick on a pig,' Paolo said as the doors closed. It was what we used to call it when we dealt with undomesticated businessmen like the Cossack – the kind of deal that, between you and me, made up half of our revenue in those days, and which not even our sanitizing covenants, undertakings, sureties and disclosures could quite perfume. It felt grubby sometimes, like a kind of legal money laundering. I used to tell myself that it would all have happened without us anyway, that we were just link men, that it wasn't us who were bankrolling whatever the Russians were going to do with the loans. Our job was just to make sure our clients would eventually get their money back. The usual lawyer's cop-out.

'Lipstick on a pig,' I agreed.

'Extreme,' said Sergei Borisovich.

I spent the rest of that afternoon in one of those distracted dazes that come over you when you have a job interview or an ominous doctor's appointment, and you nod and answer automatically when people speak to you but don't really listen. Those days when your watch seems to take a lazy age over each minute, and there is always so much time left, so little passed, since the last time you looked. And then at the end, when you're suddenly nervous and want to back out, the time goes in a rush and it's now. At about six in the evening I went home to change out of my goon suit and clean the bathroom, just in case.

| THREE

Back then, before I started avoiding him, I must have seen my neighbour Oleg Nikolaevich almost every day. I generally found him standing on the landing outside his flat when I went up or down the stairs, pretending that he wasn't waiting for me. I'd enjoyed talking to him when I first moved in and scarcely knew anyone in Moscow. He was patient with my pidgin Russian and gave me sound advice about parts of town to steer clear of. Later, when I'd settled in, it didn't cost me much to chew the fat with him for a few minutes. I felt I owed him that, and now and then it was interesting.

Oleg Nikolaevich lived alone, apart from his cat. He had a white goatee and hair in his ears. He told me once that he was the editor of a literary journal, but I wasn't sure whether it actually still existed. He was one of those careful Russian crabs that cling to the ocean floor, knowing when to hide and when to keep quiet, staying out of harm's way and trying to do none himself. He was old and lonely. He was loitering on his landing, wearing an artistic silk scarf, as I left for my dinner at Dream of the East.

'Good evening, Nikolai Ivanovich,' he said in Russian. 'How is the life of a lawyer?'

This was how Oleg Nikolaevich always greeted me. After he found out that my father's name was Ian, he started calling me Nikolai Ivanovich, which is what I would have been known as if I'd been Russian. You call people by their father's name as well as their own until you're well acquainted, and for ever with old people and your bosses. Since nobody else called me that I sort of liked it, the acceptance of me that it implied, as well as the old-school courtesy. I said I was very well and asked how he was.

'*Normalno*,' he replied. (Normal.)

I asked him to please forgive me, I was in a big hurry. I guess it must have been obvious what sort of hurry. I was doused in aftershave – the same one I sometimes use now, the one you think smells like horse piss – and I was wearing a flashy turquoise shirt that I normally saved for weddings. I'd made an inadvisable bid to slick down my hair.

'Nikolai Ivanovich!' he said, holding up a single hairy finger. I could tell that one of the Russian proverbs he loved was on the way. 'The only place with free cheese is a mousetrap.'

The odours of cat fur, decaying encyclopaedia and ageing sausage escaped from his flat and caught up with me as I hurried down the stairs, two at a time.

* * *

If I close my eyes I can watch that whole evening on the inside of my eyelids, as if it was preserved on one of those grainy old home movies from the seventies.

It was getting dark as I left home, and you could feel in the cold air that it wanted to rain. As I headed for the Bulvar from my building I saw two men sitting in the orange Zhiguli. They were not the type of men that the child would have drawn after he'd done the car. My eye caught one of theirs and I quickly looked away, as you do in London and you especially do in Moscow, where you're always seeing things through archways and in car parks or underpasses before you realize it might be better not to. I hurried up to the corner to find a taxi. The second or third passing car stopped for my outstretched arm. (I never had my own car in Russia. When I arrived, Paolo told me to start driving immediately, because if I waited till I was familiar with the anarchy and the ice and the traffic police on the roads, I never would, and he was right. But the unofficial taxi system is a surprisingly safe way to get around, so long as you obey two simple rules: don't get in if the driver's got a friend with him, and never if he's drunker than you are.)

He was Georgian, I think, my driver that night. He had two miniature icons stuck on his dashboard, little mothers of God that always made me feel safer and more vulnerable at the same time – less likely to have my throat cut, but also that my life might be in the hands of someone who thought looking in the mirror or braking were God's worries rather than his. I reached for the seat-belt, provoking a stern warning about the dangers of wearing one and assurances about his driving. He was a refugee from one of those filthy little wars that broke out in the Caucasus when the evil empire collapsed, wars that I hadn't even heard of until I started taking Moscow taxis. He started telling me about it as we plunged into the tunnel beneath the all-day traffic jam on the Novy Arbat (a broad, brutal avenue of boutiques and casinos), then accelerated past the Gogol statue. By the time we reached Kropotkinskaya Metro station and the river, and the replica cathedral that they'd thrown up there in a hurry in the nineties, both his hands were off the wheel and miming what somebody had done with someone else's body parts.

Finally he pulled up on the embankment. I gave him the hundred roubles we'd agreed on, plus a soft-touch fifty-rouble tip, and ran across the traffic to the river side of the road. Through the drizzle that was starting to fall I could see the whiteness of the space shuttle and the loops of the rickety rollercoasters in Gorky Park, on the other side of the black water. As I was crossing the little gangplank to the floating restaurant, I remember seeing a man in tight swimming trunks climbing out of the river on to the next platform along.

The restaurant was giving out that blaring restaurant din, everyone struggling to be heard above everyone else. A band in garish national dress was playing Sinatra with an Azeri twist. I was intercepted by a waitress and began to tell her that I was meeting someone there, but as I did I realized that I didn't know what name Masha would have booked under, or even whether she was really called Masha, and for a moment I thought, *What am I doing here in this crazy country in my turquoise shirt? I'm too old for this, I'm thirty-eight, I'm from Luton.* Then I saw them waving at me from the far end of the restaurant, the part that was done up to look like a medieval galleon. They stood at their table to greet me as I zigzagged across the room.

* * *

'Hello, Nicholas,' Katya said in English.

The contrast was always unsettling. Her voice sounded like

33

it belonged to a schoolgirl or a cartoon character, and yet there were the long legs in the white leather boots, bare from the knee to the hem of one of those short pleated skirts that a cheerleader or a waitress at Hooters might wear. Her blond hair was down over her shoulders. For a lot of men, I know, she would have been the main attraction, but for me she was just a little too young, a little too obvious. She was still trying them out, the walk and the hair and her curves, still seeing how far they could take her.

'Hello, Nikolai,' said Masha. She was wearing a miniskirt that almost matched my shirt and a comparatively demure black jumper. Lipstick and mascara, but not too clownish like some of the others. Blood-red nails.

I sat down opposite them. At the table behind me were half a dozen noisy businessmen, and with them seven or eight women who were young enough to be their daughters but weren't.

Naturally there was nothing much to say.

We looked down for longer than we needed to at the menus, with their time-consuming lists of meats and sauces (and next to them two columns of numbers: the prices, and also, as in most Moscow restaurants, the weight of the ingredients in each dish, an up-front detail supposed to reassure diners that they weren't being ripped off). I remember how my eye involuntarily tripped on the prices for the Shashlik Royale and the Sea Surprise. Singledom can turn you frugal, even when you are flush.

'So, Kolya,' Masha finally said in English, using one of those cutesy Russian diminutives. 'Why did you come to our Russia?'

'Let's speak Russian,' I said. 'I think it will be easier.'

'Please,' Katya said. 'We need practice for our English.'

'Okay,' I said. I hadn't gone to Dream of the East to argue with them. After that we mostly stuck to English, except when we were with other Russians.

'*Tak*,' Katya said. 'So. Why to Russia?'

I gave the easy answer I always did when asked that question: 'I wanted an adventure.'

That wasn't really true. The reason, I can see now, is that I found myself entering the thirty-something zone of disappointment, the time when momentum and ambition start to fade and friends' parents start to die. The time of 'Is that all there is?' People I knew in London who had already got married began to get divorced, and people who hadn't adopted cats. People started running marathons or becoming Buddhists to help them get through it. For you I guess it was those dodgy evangelical seminars you once told me you went to a couple of times before we met. The truth is, the firm asked me if I'd go out to Moscow, just for a year, they said, maybe two. It was a short cut to a partnership, they hinted. I said yes, and ran away from London and how young I wasn't any more.

They smiled.

I said, 'My company asked me to come to the Moscow office. It was a good opportunity for me. Also,' I added, 'I'd always wanted to come to Russia. My grandfather was in Russia during the war.'

That part was true, as you know. I never knew him properly, but his war record came up all the time when I was a kid.

'Where did your grandfather serve?' Masha asked. 'Was he spy?'

'No,' I said. 'He was a sailor. He was on the convoys – you know, the ships that brought supplies to Russia from England. He was on the convoys to the Arctic. To Arkhangelsk. And to Murmansk.'

Masha leaned over and murmured something to Katya, which I thought was a translation.

'Really?' she said. 'No jokes? He was in Murmansk?'

'Yes. More than once. He was lucky. His ship was never hit. I think he wanted to go back to Russia after the war. But they were Soviet times and it wasn't possible. My father told me all this – my grandfather died when I was young.'

'This for us is interesting,' said Katya. 'Because we are from this city. Murmansk is our home.'

Just then the waiter arrived to take our order. They both asked for sturgeon shashlik. I ordered lamb, plus some of the Azeri pancakes that they stuff with cheese and herbs, the little aubergine rolls filled with a walnut mush, some pomegranate sauce and half a bottle of vodka.

At the time my grandfather having been in their home town seemed an important coincidence or clue. I asked them why their family had lived up there. I knew Murmansk had been one of the special restricted military cities, where you only wound up if you had a reason, or if someone else had a reason for you.

Masha looked me in the eyes and tapped the red nails of her right hand on her shoulder. I thought I was supposed to say or do something in response, but I didn't know what. After a few seconds I tapped my hand on my shoulder too. They laughed, Masha throwing her head back, Katya doing one of those suppressed blushing laughs that can keep you out of trouble at school when you crack up during lessons.

'No,' said Masha. 'What is it called, this thing that men in army have?' She tapped again.

'Epaulettes?' I said.

'When one Russian makes this,' she said, still tapping, 'it means man who is in army, or can be police or one of others.'

'Your father?'

'Yes,' she said. 'He was sailor. His father also was sailor. Like your grandfather.'

'Yes,' said Katya. 'Our grandfather was fighting next to convoys also. Maybe they were knowing each other.'

'Maybe,' I said.

We smiled. We fidgeted. I looked at Masha and away when she caught me, that first-date cat-and-mouse. Behind the girls, through the steamed-up window and the rain that had begun to fall into the river, I could just make out the quiet park rides, and the Krimsky Bridge, and beyond that the glow of the giant ridiculous statue of Peter the Great that stands in the river near the Red October chocolate factory.

I asked them about growing up in Murmansk. Of course it was hard, Masha said. Of course it was not Moscow. But in the summer it was light around the clock, and you could go walking in the forest in the middle of the night.

'And we have one of this!' Katya said, pointing towards the ribs of the Ferris wheel in Gorky Park. She smiled again, and she seemed to me a harmless innocent girl, who thought a Ferris wheel was like Disney World.

'Only,' said Masha, 'it was too expensive. To ride. When I was small girl, in eighties, during Gorbachev, I could only look at it, this wheel. I thought it was too beautiful.'

I asked, 'Why did you leave? Why did you come to Moscow?'

I thought I already knew the answer. Most of the provincial Russian girls came to the city with just enough money to look good on for a couple of weeks, while they slept on someone's floor and tried to find a job, or ideally a man, who could whisk them off to live behind the electric fences on the 'elitny' Rublovskoe Shosse. Or maybe, if he was already married, he would install her in an apartment on the streets around Patriarshie Prudy – Patriarch's Ponds: the Hampstead of Moscow, with more automatic weapons – where he'd only bother her twice a week and let her keep the place when he got bored with her. In those days, leggy desperate girls were Russia's main national product, after oil. You could order them on the internet in Leeds or Minneapolis.

'Because of family,' said Masha.

'Your parents moved to Moscow?'

'No,' she said. 'Parents stay in Murmansk. But I must move.'

She made another gesture, one that this time I understood. She raised her hand again and flicked the side of her white neck with her index finger. Drink. The all-Russia sign for drink.

'Your father?'

'Yes.'

I imagined the rows and the tears up there in Murmansk, and the wages drunk in pay-day binges, and the little girls hiding

39

in their bedroom, dreaming of the big wheel they couldn't afford to ride.

'Now,' said Masha, 'only mother is living.'

I wasn't sure whether or not to say I was sorry.

'But,' said Katya, 'in Moscow we also have family.'

'Yes,' said Masha, 'in Moscow we are not alone. We have aunt. Maybe you meet her. She is old communist. I think for you it will be interesting.'

I said, 'I would love to meet your aunt.'

'In Murmansk,' Masha said, 'we knew nothing. Everything we learned in Moscow. Everything good. And also everything bad.'

They brought all the dishes at once, as they always do in Caucasian restaurants, never much valuing the deferred gratification implicit in the starter/main course concept. We ate. Behind us the businessmen had given up on the food to paw at their companions, not very surreptitiously. Their table was an orgy of smoking. I imagine they smoked in the shower.

I tried to find out where Masha and Katya lived. They said they rented a place out on the Leningradskoe Shosse, the choked highway that leads to Sheremetyevo airport and the north. I asked Masha whether she enjoyed her job at the mobile phone shop.

'It is work,' Masha said. 'It is not always interesting.' She gave me a short ironic smile.

'What do you do, Katya?'

'I study MGU,' she said. MGU meant Moscow State University, Russia's version of Oxford, but with bribes to get in and then out again with a degree. 'I study business management,' she said.

I was impressed, as I was supposed to be. I started to tell them about my own college years in Birmingham, but Masha interrupted me.

'Let's dance,' she said.

The band was playing 'I Will Survive' at double speed, the musicians sounding like massed mourners at a Caucasian funeral when they joined in with the chorus. The only other dancers were an excited child and the tipsy father she had dragged out into the space in front of the band. Masha and Katya were all curves and pelvic thrusts, with a dash of the simulated lesbianism that was then de rigueur on Moscow dance floors, unselfconscious as only people with nothing to lose can be. That was something else about Masha that I liked: she could just be in the moment, cutting it off from before and afterwards in order to be happy.

I shuffled and jerked, tried a little twist, then felt maybe I'd overdone it (I know I have to go to those lessons before we do our number on the day, I haven't forgotten). Masha took my hand and we did a couple of minutes of sub-ballroom stumble, me clinging on to her for cover. I was relieved when we made it to the end of the song and could retreat to the table.

'You are beautiful dancer,' said Katya, and they laughed.

'To the women!' I said, a standard fall-back toast, and since in Russia the toastee drinks too, they clinked their stumpy vodka glasses against mine and we drank.

I still wasn't sure what the proposition was, if there was one, and if it wasn't just curiosity and the chance of a free dinner. In Moscow the main event was usually the third date, like for us in London – I expect like on Mars – or maybe the second in the summer. I didn't know what was supposed to happen with Katya.

'Maybe you want to see our photos?' Masha asked me.

She nodded at Katya, who brought out her mobile phone. They loved photographing each other, the girls in Russia – something about the novelty of the cameras, I think, and the idea that they might matter enough to have their pictures taken.

'From Odessa,' Katya said. They had been there at the beginning of the summer, they explained. They had a relative there, apparently. More or less everyone seemed to have a relative in Odessa (a sort of cross between Tenerife and Palermo).

We leaned into the middle of the table, and Katya gave us a slide show on the tiny screen of her phone. In the first photo they were in a bar, the two of them and another girl. Katya was looking away from the camera and laughing, like she was sharing a joke with someone out of the picture. In the second one they were on the beach, standing next to each other in bikinis, with what looked like an Egyptian pyramid behind them. The next was just Masha. It showed her taking a picture of her reflection in a wardrobe mirror: she was standing with one hand on her hip, the other hand holding the phone so it obscured a quarter of her face. In the mirror she was wearing red bikini knickers and nothing else.

I sat back in my chair and asked whether they'd like to come to my apartment for some tea.

Masha looked hard into my eyes and said yes.

I waved at the waiter and wrote a little squiggle in the air with an imaginary pen, the international let-me-out-of-here signal that, when you're a teenager and see your parents make it, you think you never will.

* * *

When we got outside it was colder. After three winters in Russia I knew this was the real thing: the big chill, the ice in the air that stays till April. The white smoke from the power plant down the river was congealed against the thick night. It was still drizzling, the droplets sliding down my glasses and blurring my vision, making everything seem even more fantastical than it already did. Masha was wearing her cat-fur coat, and Katya had put on a purple plastic raincoat.

I stuck out my arm for a lift, and a car that was already twenty metres past us braked and reversed back up the street and into the kerb. The driver asked for two hundred roubles, and even though it was daylight robbery I agreed and got into the front seat. He was a fat resentful Russian, with a moustache and a crack in the middle of his windscreen that looked like it had been made by a forehead, or a bullet. He had a miniature television jerry-rigged up to the cigarette lighter, and he carried on watching a dubbed Brazilian soap opera as he drove us along the river. Ahead of us were the throbbing stars on top of the Kremlin towers and the fairy-tale domes of St Basil's at the back of Red Square, and next to us the soupy Moscow River, not yet frozen and curling mysteriously through the wild city. Behind me Masha and Katya were whispering to each other. The fat Russian's car was a mobile heaven, a ten-minute paradise of hope and amazement.

* * *

If you looked closely at the ceiling of my flat you could just make out a grid of intersecting creases, which told the apartment's history like the rings of a tree trunk or the wrinkles

44

on a poet's face. It had been a *kommunalka*, a communal flat in which three or four families had lived together but separately. I used to imagine how people must have died and been discovered by their flatmates, or had died and not been discovered. Like millions of others they must have taken their individual toilet seats down from the wall when they went to crap, argued about the milk in the communal kitchen, informed on each other and saved each other. Then in the nineties someone had knocked through all the old bedroom partitions and turned the whole place into a rich man's pad, and from that past life only the lines on the ceiling where the walls used to meet it were left. There were only two bedrooms now, one for the guests who almost never came, and the bad history and my good luck made me feel guilty, at least to begin with.

They took off their shoes in the way Russians are trained to and we went through into the kitchen. Masha sat on my lap and kissed me. Her lips were cold and strong. I looked over at Katya and she was smiling. I knew they might be taking me for something but there was nothing in my apartment that I wanted more than I wanted Masha, and I didn't think they'd kill me. She took my hand and led me to my bedroom.

I went to the window to close the curtains – they were a sort of rich ruched brown, and looked as if they should have opened to reveal an opera set – and when I turned round Masha had taken off her jumper and was sitting on the edge of my bed in her short skirt and a black bra. Katya was sitting in a chair, smiling. She never did it again, but that night she sat there all the way through, maybe for security, I don't know. It was kinkily disconcerting, but then the whole thing felt surreal, and the vodka took the edge off.

Masha was different from girls in England. Different from you. Different from me too. Less polite about it, less like she was acting or pretending. She had a kind of basic earthy energy, gripping and encouraging and laughing, keen to please and to improvise. Whenever I looked up Katya was just there, grinning, close enough for me to see even without my glasses, fully clothed like she was watching a science experiment.

Afterwards, when we were spooning and Masha was breathing heavily, not awake but not all asleep, she shook the hand I had stretched across her to hold her hand as if it was a defective toy – to make me hold her more tightly, or to prove that it and me were real, as if the hand and me were things she needed. Or that's how it seemed to me then. At the other end of the bed, part of us but also miles away, she hooked her leg around my leg, I remember, so I could just feel the painted toenails of her white foot digging into my calf.

When the light crept into my bedroom in the morning I saw Katya asleep in the chair, her knees curled up under her chin, still dressed, her blond hair spread over her face like a veil. Masha was lying next to me, with her face turned away, her hair on my pillow and her smell on my skin. I fell asleep again, and when I woke up a second time they had both gone.

| FOUR

'This is it,' Masha said.

We were standing outside a classic old Moscow building, with a cracked pastel façade and a wide courtyard where the nobility would once have kept their horses and their plotting servants. Now the courtyard contained two unhappy trees with drooping brown leaves and three or four cars, chichi enough to make it clear that money was in residence. We went through the arch from the street, and across to a metal doorway with a vintage intercom in the far left-hand corner of the yard. The air was wet – heavy with something that isn't sleet and isn't quite snow, a Russian humidity that tastes of exhaust fumes and seeps into your eyes and mouth. It was the kind of Moscow weather that makes you want the sky to just get on with it, like a condemned prisoner looking up at the blade of the guillotine.

Masha punched in the number of the flat. There was a pause, then a crackly buzz. A woman's voice said, '*Da?*'

'It's us,' said Masha in Russian. 'Masha, Katya and Nikolai.'

'Come up,' said the voice. 'Third floor.'

She buzzed us in and we climbed the stained marble stairs.

'She was once communist,' said Masha, 'but now I think she is not.'

'She is sometimes forgetting things,' Katya said, 'but she is very kind.'

'I think she is not so happy,' Masha said. 'But we try.'

She was waiting for us on the landing. She had one of those miniature shot-putter babushka figures, and a face that looked younger than her grey hair, which she'd trimmed into a pragmatic Soviet bowl. She was wearing lace-up black shoes, tan stockings and a neat but worn woollen skirt and cardigan that told you straight off that the money didn't live with her. She had clever eyes and a nice smile.

'Dear one,' said Masha, 'this is Nikolai...' I saw her realizing that she didn't know my surname. It was, I think, only the fourth time we'd seen each other, not including the first day on the Metro. We were strangers, really, perhaps we were always strangers. But at the time it felt right, being introduced to her aunt. It felt like we might last.

'Platt,' I said, and then still in Russian as we shook hands, 'Very pleased to meet you.'

'Come in,' she said, smiling.

I am getting ahead of myself, I'm afraid. But I wanted to tell you how I met her – how I met Tatiana Vladimirovna, the old lady.

* * *

In those gold-rush days – when half the buildings in the centre of the city were covered in submarine-sized Rolex adverts, and apartments in Stalin's wedding-cake skyscrapers were going for Knightsbridge prices – money in Moscow had its own particular habits. Money knew that someone in the Kremlin might decide to take it back at any moment. It didn't relax over coffee or promenade with three-wheeled buggies in Hyde Park like London money does. Moscow money emigrated to the Cayman Islands, villas on Cap Ferrat or anywhere else that would give it a warm home and ask no questions. Or it combusted itself as conspicuously as possible, poured itself into champagne-filled jacuzzis and took flight in private helicopters. Money especially loved the top-end car dealerships along Kutuzovsky Prospekt, on the way out to the war museum and Victory Park. It decorated its Mercs and fortified Hummers with flashing blue emergency lights, dispensed for thirty thousand dollars or so by obliging officials at the interior ministry, lights that parted the Moscow gridlock like the seas of Egypt. The cars congregated around the must-be-seen-in restaurants and nightclubs like basking predators at watering holes, while money went inside to gorge itself on caviar and Cristal champagne.

On a Friday night at the sharp end of October – two or three weeks before I was introduced to Tatiana Vladimirovna at the door of her apartment, I guess about the same length of time after my first night with Masha – I took the two girls to Rasputin. It was then one of the city's most elitny nightclubs, on a corner between the Hermitage Gardens and the police station on Petrovka (the station where they film the Russian version of *Crimestoppers*, embellished with corpses and considerately staged shoot-outs). At least, I tried to take them to Rasputin.

We weaved through the pride of parked, tinted-window automotive monsters to the entrance. It was fortified by agents of what Muscovites call *feis kontrol*: two or three Himalayan bouncers and a haughty blonde wearing a headset, whose job it was to keep out insufficiently glamorous women and under-salaried men. The blonde looked the girls up and down in the frankly competitive way that Russian women do. Katya was wearing a leopard-print miniskirt above her white boots, and I remember Masha had her long hair in a sort of tousled mane, and a silver bracelet with a miniature watch in the shape of a heart attached. I think it was my fault that they stopped us. I was trying to fit in with the mafia ambience by wearing my dark work suit and a black shirt, but I probably looked like a member of the chorus in some school production of *Guys and Dolls*. I could see the woman on the door guessing how much pain I could call down if I got angry, estimating the seriousness of my *krisha* – the protective human 'roof' that every Russian needs, preferably in one of the security services, if they want to get off the hook, into a lower tax bracket or into Rasputin on a Friday night. From the market trader with his friendly policeman who looks the other way, to the oligarch with his obliging Kremlin overlord, anyone who wants to prosper needs a *krisha*: someone to bend an ear or twist an arm, a relative maybe, or an old friend, or just someone powerful whose compromising secrets you are lucky enough to know. The woman whispered something to one of the bouncers, who ushered us around a corner into a roped-off line of rejects. We might be admitted later, he told us, if there was room for us among the A-listers.

It was snowing. It was light, October snow, the type Russians call *mokri sneg*, damp snow, which settles on kind surfaces like the branches of trees and the roofs of cars, but is obliterated when it hits the unfriendly Moscow pavements. Some of the flakes weren't making it that far, getting caught in up-gusts as they passed the tops of lampposts, pirouetting up again in the artificial light as if they had reconsidered. It was cold – not seriously cold, not yet, but flirting with zero. The other people in our rejects' line drew their hands up into their sleeves, making them look like a race of amputees. Assorted gangsters, off-duty colonels from the security service and mid-range officials from the Ministry of Finance were waved through by the bouncers, each trailing a high-heeled personal harem. I was cross and embarrassed, and ready to give up and leave. Then the Cossack arrived.

He was with two or three other men and four tall girls. I called out to him, and he hung back behind his friends as they went through the velvet curtains on the door. It was one of those moments when parts of your life that are supposed to be strangers collide, like running into your boss in the foyer of a cinema or the changing rooms of a swimming pool.

'Good evening,' he said. He was talking to me but looking at the girls. 'Not bad.'

'Good evening,' I said.

I'd seen the Cossack again a couple of days before. He came to Paveletskaya to sign papers, make promises and burp. He'd agreed to our appointment of a surveyor, who was to visit the site of the oil terminal every few weeks and confirm that construction was on schedule. That would help to prove that the repayments would eventually be met, and that, as the contract we'd drawn up provided for in lavish detail, there would be something for the banks to repossess if the Cossack and his friends ever defaulted. The surveyor we briefed was a little mole of a man called Vyacheslav Alexandrovich. We'd worked with him before, on the finance for a port development down on the Black Sea coast.

'Aren't you going to introduce me?'

'Excuse me,' I said. 'These are my friends, Masha and Katya.'

'*Enchanté*,' said the Cossack. 'Which one of you is Nicholas's wife?'

He'd rumbled the little lie I'd told him about being married, but he didn't seem to mind. I blushed. Katya giggled. Masha shook his hand. It was the only time they met, as far as I know, and in a way I'm pleased they did. It simplifies things for me, somehow, that memory of Masha and the Cossack together.

'Do you have a problem?' he asked me.

'No,' I said.

'Yes,' Masha corrected. She was always calm, determined, self-assured. Always. I liked that about her too.

'Maybe,' I said.

'Just a second,' said the Cossack.

He walked over to the blonde with the headset. He had his

back to us so I couldn't see his expression. But I saw his shoulder blade twitch in our direction and the woman look over at us. He kept talking and her face fell, then her head dropped, and she spoke into her headset and beckoned towards me.

The Cossack said, 'Enjoy yourselves!'

You know the way, in action films sometimes, they show how soldiers look when they're seen through night-vision goggles – edged in a sort of shimmering thermal glow? The Cossack looked like that all the time, I think. He was outlined in violence. It was invisible but everyone could see it.

'Thanks,' I said.

'It's nothing,' replied the Cossack.

We shook hands, and he kept hold of me for just a moment too long, a couple of seconds maybe, so I knew he could. 'Say hi to my friend Paolo,' he said.

Inside there was a dance floor with three podium dancers – two energetic and topless black girls, and in between them a male dwarf wearing a tiger-stripe thong. Katya pointed up at the ceiling. Two naked girls, sprayed gold to look like cherubs and with wings attached, were flapping above our heads. We headed for the bar. It had a glass floor, and underneath it there was an aquarium filled with sturgeon and a few forlorn sharks. There were a lot of priceless women and dangerous men.

I ordered three mojitos from a barman wearing the underpaid, harassed frown of barmen on a busy night everywhere, plus a round of the risky sushi that was then standard-issue across Moscow nightspots. I felt like a lottery winner, sitting in Rasputin with the high rollers and their surgically enhanced molls – me with my pointless thick hair and pinched English features, and a new mid-thirties pad of flesh around my jaw that I looked for in the mirror every morning, in the hope that it might have gone away of its own accord. I felt like I was some-body, instead of the nobody who could at that moment have been flowing over London Bridge with all the others. I guess that's how I was supposed to feel.

Katya asked me more about England. The usual questions: Was Sherlock Holmes real? Was it hard to get a visa? Why did Churchill wait until 1944 to open a second front? She was a good kid, I thought, inside the micro-mini, deferential to her sister, keen to get on in an understandably narrow way.

Masha asked me about my job.

'Kolya,' she said, 'do you know only English law or Russian law also?'

I said I was trained in English law but understood Russian law well enough too, especially corporate law.

'What sort of deals are you doing?'

I said it was mostly loans, and the odd merger or acquisition.

'It means you are not working on deals for property?' Her

voice was almost smothered by the cardiac beat of the Russki dance music and the cawing of thugs.

I said no, I wasn't. I knew a little about property law, but not much – only really the parts covering long leases for commercial buildings.

I know I should have thought harder than I did about those questions. But I was busy thinking about Masha, and going back to my place, and whether this was what the famous 'real thing' felt like.

* * *

Katya said she had a birthday party to go to. I said we'd escort her, but she said no, she was fine, and hurried off alone in the direction of the Bolshoi Theatre, into the early snow and the unruly Russian night.

I suggested getting a cab, but Masha said she wanted to walk. We walked back up towards Pushkin Square: past the pretty church that the communists had spared, and on the left the strip club at the side of the Pushkin Cinema (where a group of Hungarian businessmen got cremated in the upstairs cubicles a few months later), and opposite that a casino with a sports car outside, in a tilted glass case. Through the damp snow the city seemed to soften, the edges of the buildings fading out like in an Impressionist painting. Ahead of us the neon of the square, with its all-you-can-eat restaurants and statue of the famous poet, glowed like some gaudy Mongol encampment.

Masha told me that night how she worried about Katya, how apart from their aunt it was just the two of them in Moscow, how they'd always dreamed of coming but how difficult it was. She'd had to come up with five hundred dollars to get her job, she said, the normal recruitment bribe for the manager of her shop, and it had taken her six months to pay off the money she'd had to borrow. She said she hoped that maybe one day she would live somewhere safer, somewhere cleaner.

'Like London,' I said. 'Maybe like London.' I was going too fast, I know, especially compared to how it's been between me and you. But somehow the idea didn't seem outlandish, not at the beginning. I am trying to be honest with you. I think that's the best thing for both of us now.

'Maybe,' she said. She took my hand as we went down the slippery steps into the underpass where we'd met and kept holding it after we reached the bottom.

Up on the other side of Tverskaya we walked for a while along the middle of the Bulvar. The city authorities had pulled the flowers out of their beds, as they do every year when the game is up, carting them away in the night like condemned prisoners so they don't die in public. The Russians had put on their intermediate coats, the women in the wool or leopard-print numbers they mostly wear until it's time for their mothballed furs. On the benches the tramps lay seasoned with snow, like meat sprinkled with salt on a butcher's slab. In my street the bonnet of the rusty Zhiguli was freckled with melting snowflakes.

When we got inside Masha put on a CD, took off her coat, then, slowly, and like she'd done it to music before, everything else too.

Afterwards she ran a bath. She squeezed in behind me, her groomed pubic hair bristling against my coccyx, and wrapped her long legs around my loose belly. She had a front-row view of the copses of hairs on my shoulders and the top left corner of my back, those asymmetrical practical jokes played by my genes that you're not all that keen on. She half sang, half hummed a weepy Russian folk song, running her wet fingers through my hair. It felt to me like a new kind of nakedness, our bodies limp and open rather than exhibits or weapons. Slopping in the water with each other felt like honesty, and the streaked fake-marble tub, with the jet-stream valves that didn't work, felt like our little womb.

She told me in the bath, I remember, about how proud she'd been of her father when she was a little girl, but how things had changed when the old empire died and his salary had stopped being paid. That was when the serious drinking started, she said. She told me about how, when she was very young, she'd been taught at school to revere some Stalin-era brat who'd informed on his own father for hoarding grain. They'd sung songs about him and drawn pictures of him, this little Siberian sod, until one day their teacher had told them to stop singing the songs and to tear up the pictures, and that was how she knew that something terrible had happened.

'Didn't you feel free?' I asked her. 'When communism ended, didn't you feel free?'

'In Murmansk,' she replied, 'we felt only poor. And cold. People said, "Freedom we cannot eat."'

She told me that when she was seventeen her mother had needed an operation. As with everything else that was theoretically provided by the government, from the midwife who brought you into the world to your burial plot, they'd had to pay – had to bribe the doctor and buy the medicines, the soap and the sutures to sew her up afterwards. So Masha had left college only a week after she'd started, she said, to work in the canteen at the naval base. She still sent money back to her mother every month. My guess had been close: she was twenty-four, she said, and Katya was twenty.

I asked her how she felt about it all – leaving school, going to work, sacrificing her chances for her mother.

'It was normal,' she said. 'You know, Kolya, in those times we weren't having such big hopes. Bad food. Bad men. Bad luck. This was not surprise.'

It was the right combination that she was offering, of course, with her strength and her misfortune. She was tough and worldly, somehow older than me as well as much younger (though by Moscow standards the age gap was respectable). At the same time she seemed powerless and almost alone. She tapped the right mix of needs: the need to save someone, or think you can, that I reckon all men feel somewhere, and the need to be saved.

I knew I didn't have the kind of money she'd probably been hoping for. But I thought I could offer her security.

I asked her what sort of ship her father had served on. She said she wasn't supposed to tell anyone, especially not a foreigner. Then she laughed loudly and said it probably didn't matter any more.

'He was on boat – how do you say? – boat against ice. To make path for other boats.'

'Ice-breaker.'

'Yes,' she said, 'ice-breaker. He was on atomic ice-breaker. My grandfather also was on ice-breaker. In war he was helping to break ice for western ships. For your grandfather maybe.'

'What was the ship's name? Your father's, I mean.' I thought that was another question you should ask about sailors.

She said she wasn't sure, she'd forgotten. But she thought for a few seconds and said, '*Petrograd*. Ice-breaker was called *Petrograd*. Because of revolution.' She smiled, the way you might if you'd dredged up a lost but precious fact out of your memory.

In the morning, when she was still asleep, with her head in profile on the pillow, I found a small crook two-thirds of the way up her nose, invisible from the front – the result, I guessed, of a fatherly backhander or a rough sailor boyfriend. I found matching dark freckles in the middles of the moon-white cheeks of her arse. And I noticed the tiny creases that were just appearing at the corners of her eyes. I remember how those lines made me want her even more, because they made her real, a physical thing that could die, but not only die.

Later, when we were drinking our tea with lemon slices in the kitchen – Ikea mugs, Ikea chairs, most of my flat was from Ikea, which was by then as inevitable in Moscow as death and tax-evasion (and cirrhosis) – she told me again about her aunt, the one who lived in Moscow. She told me that she and Katya saw her as often as they could but not as much as they should. She said she would like to introduce me soon.

'Maybe next week,' she said. 'Or week after next week. She is alone in Moscow and comes happy when we visit. She will like you. I think she is not knowing many foreigners. Maybe none. Please.'

Yes, I said. Of course I would meet her aunt. Masha drank her tea, kissed me on the nose and went to work.

* * *

It was approaching the middle of November. All the *mokri sneg* had melted, but some of the ice that had formed during the October cold snap survived, retreating into the cracks in the pavements and wounds in the roads like trapped platoons waiting for reinforcements. Tatiana Vladimirovna said, 'Come in.'

Say what you like about the Soviets, they were the all-time world champions of parquet. It stretched away from the plain front door of her apartment in interlocking Khrushchev-era boomerangs, interrupted in the middle of the floor by a faded Turkmen rug. There was a glittery communist chandelier, which looked fabulous so long as you didn't get too close to it.

We took off our shoes, hung up our coats and followed Tatiana Vladimirovna down the corridor. I can remember her apartment much better than I'd like to. We passed a bedroom with two single beds, only one of them made up, plus a dark wooden wardrobe and a white dressing table with an ornamental mirror. There was another room half full of packing boxes, then the door of the bathroom and a kitchen with tired linoleum and a primitive fridge. The lounge she led us to was covered in a kind of hairy brown wallpaper, peeling a little in one corner where it met the ceiling, with a bookshelf full of old Soviet encyclopaedias and reports and a big wooden desk covered in green baize. On the desk was the kind of Russian party spread I always dreaded, as inedible as it was extravagant. It had probably cost her about a month's pension and a fortnight's cooking, all sweaty fish, jellied and unidentifiable bits of animals, Russian chocolate broken into clumps, blinis that were getting cold, sour cream and a special sweet cheese they fry in little rolls.

The windows were closed and the central heating – still controlled centrally by the city government, like in the old days – was inhuman. Tatiana Vladimirovna gestured us towards a moulting sofa. 'Tea,' she said, a statement not a question, and left.

The girls sat down to whisper. I got up and poked around. Tatiana Vladimirovna's place overlooked the Bulvar and the pond at Chistie Prudy ('Clean Ponds' – typical Russian wishful thinking as far as the water was concerned, but an increasingly smart part of central Moscow). She had a big window that faced across the pond and the trees that flanked it. They'd packed away the Bedouin-tent-style restaurant that was set up on a platform over the water in summer, and the gondolas that offered overpriced serenades had been beached. On the other side of the pond was a strange blue building decorated with reliefs of real and imaginary animals, one of the beautiful things you sometimes trip over in that city, like flowers on a battlefield. I could make out owls, pelicans, double-headed griffins, two-tongued crocodiles, pouncing but somehow despondent hounds. The confused November sky reminded me of a black-and-white television set that hasn't been tuned in.

On one wall of the room there was a set of plates, with the classic blue and gold St Petersburg pattern, and a certificate from a technical college in Novosibirsk. There was an old Bakelite-style radio, a faux mahogany contraption as big as a trunk that opened at the top. Two framed black and white photos sat on the bookshelf. One showed a young couple perching on some windy rocks by the sea, she laughing and looking at him, he prematurely balding, wearing serious spectacles and looking into the camera. The couple looked happy in a way that I didn't think people in the Soviet Union were supposed to have been happy. In the bottom right-hand corner of the picture, in stencilled white lettering, it said, 'Yalta, 1956'. The other photo showed a girl stretching herself across the diameter of a sort of outsized hamster wheel, her hands clutching the rim, apparently taking part in a synchronized gymnastics routine:

two more wheels with girls inside them jutted into the picture. When I crooked my head and looked closely I could see that the angled figure was the same slim girl as in the beach photo, maybe a few years younger, wearing tennis-style shorts that were sexier than they were probably meant to be and a wide fixed grin. It was her, my bent head finally understood. It was Tatiana Vladimirovna.

Behind the buffet on the desk was another photo, showing the man with the glasses, now a little older, sitting at the same desk, which in the photo was covered with orderly papers, an ashtray and an old-fashioned rotary telephone. He had half turned from his work to face the photographer, as if the work was too important to forget about altogether.

'That is my husband,' said Tatiana Vladimirovna in Russian. She was standing behind me with a small silver samovar in her hands. 'That is Pyotr Arkadyevich.'

She made tea in the Russian way, pouring superstrong dark shots from a teapot, then topping them up with steaming water from the samovar. She gave us each a little saucer of jam, and teaspoons to dip in it so we could eat the jam with the tea, alternating sips and slurps in a way that I could never quite get the hang of.

We talked. Some of the conversation felt like a job interview, some of it like a tourist-board guide to Russian geography.

'What is your profession, Nikolai?'

'I am a lawyer.'

'What is your father's profession?'

'He is a teacher. My mother is also a teacher. But now they are retired.'

'Do you like Moscow?'

'Yes, I like it very much.'

'And apart from Moscow, where have you been in our Russia?'

I said I'd been to one or two of the monastery towns near Moscow, I'd forgotten their names, I was sorry.

Hadn't I been to Siberia to see 'our great Lake Baikal'? Did I know it was the biggest lake in the world? Did I know that there were eleven kinds of salmon in the rivers of Kamchatka?

I switched on to auto-pilot. My eyes kept flitting towards the arc of Masha's thigh. And then, as old Russians often do, Tatiana Vladimirovna mentioned something that made me feel infinitely naïve, born yesterday in comparison to what she'd lived through and seen – an extreme version of how you feel when you're twelve, and your parents talk incomprehensibly about taxes or somebody getting divorced. In Russia it might be how uncle such-and-such went to the Gulag and didn't come back, or just some humdrum everyday heroism or indignity – how someone shared a room with his parents till he was forty, or used to have her mail censored or stand in three-day queues for potatoes.

She asked me if I'd been to St Petersburg. I said no, not yet, but that my mother was planning to visit me, soon maybe (it was true, she was threatening to), and that we were hoping to go there together.

'I am from St Petersburg,' she said. 'From Leningrad. I was born in a village near Leningrad.'

In the village, she went on, her mother had milked cows and prayed in secret. Her father worked on a collective farm. They'd moved to the city after he died, Tatiana Vladimirovna said, just before the Great Patriotic War, when she was seven or eight years old. She lost a sister and her mother in the siege. An elder brother, she told me, still smiling, had been killed at the Battle of Kursk. Some years after the war she'd gone with her new husband, the man in the photos, to Novosibirsk, a university town in Siberia. It was strange, she said, in Siberia they felt almost free, more than in Leningrad before the war or in Moscow later. Her husband was a scientist and – here my Russian threatened to give out, though I'm not sure my English would have been up to it either – I think he helped to design a paint that went inside missile silos, or something like that, and was tough enough, she said, to resist the heat when the missiles took off.

'He was big scientist,' said Katya in English.

'That is why Tatiana Vladimirovna has this apartment in the centre of Moscow,' Masha said in Russian. 'For services to the fatherland.'

'Yes,' said Tatiana Vladimirovna. 'Comrade Khrushchev gave my husband the apartment in 1962. It was a major worry at that time, how to launch the missiles without burning the silos. Pyotr Arkadyevich worked very hard and in the end he found the answer.'

She herself still worked, she said, as a part-time guide at a museum near Gorky Park, dedicated to some famous Russian scientist I hadn't heard of. She had the deference that old people sometimes show towards the young, racing through her life story so as not to take up too much of our precious youthful time. I liked Tatiana Vladimirovna. I liked her immediately, and I liked her right till the end.

'So, Nikolai,' she said, 'what do you think of our little scheme?'

I had absolutely no idea what she was talking about. I glanced at Masha. She uncrossed her legs and nodded.

'I think it's an excellent scheme,' I said, wanting to please.

'Yes,' Tatiana Vladimirovna said. 'Excellent.'

We all smiled.

'Nikolai!' said Tatiana Vladimirovna, jumping up and changing the subject. 'Girls! You haven't eaten anything.'

We all cooed around the desk, where Tatiana Vladimirovna handed out the plates and saw to it that I got the fish I didn't like. I made sure I had enough cold blinis to hide it under.

We sat down. Tatiana Vladimirovna asked Katya about university.

'It is hard work,' Katya said, 'but very interesting.'

We drifted into a well-meaning but awkward silence.

'Fish loves to swim!' Tatiana Vladimirovna exclaimed. She got to her feet, went to the kitchen and came back with an unopened bottle of vodka and four old shot glasses with snowflakes etched into them. She poured, and we all stood up to clink our glasses.

'To your success, kids!' said Tatiana Vladimirovna, and knocked back her vodka in the efficient Russian way.

The three of us drank too. I felt the vodka at the back of my throat, then in my stomach, and after that the warmth in my chest and the instant elation that made it such a curse. I felt the colour in my cheeks, and the liver damage and indiscretions that were on their way. I hadn't troubled to ask anyone what the scheme was.

Ten minutes later ('To Russia!' 'To us!' 'To the Queen of England!'), I asked Masha in English whether she was ready to go. She said no, she needed to talk to Tatiana Vladimirovna. I knew it might be rude to leave before the bottle was empty, but

70

I told Tatiana Vladimirovna that unfortunately I had a meeting to get to.

'But you haven't eaten anything,' she protested, looking at my over-worked plate and clasping her hands in front of her.

I said, 'I'm sorry.' I said it had been a great pleasure to meet her.

I kissed both girls on the cheek. Tatiana Vladimirovna followed me as I swam across the parquet to put on my coat and shoes.

'Goodbye,' I said. 'Enormous thanks. Until we meet again.'

'You haven't eaten anything,' she repeated as she shut the door behind me. I bolted down the stairs, escaping the heavy suffocating childlessness.

* * *

Later that day I found Oleg Nikolaevich standing on the half landing between our floors, wearing a black suit and shirt and a black trilby. He was darkly immaculate, apart from a couple of stray cat hairs on his lapel. He seemed to have trimmed his beard. He looked like he was going to his own funeral.

'How are you, Oleg Nikolaevich?' I think I was still a little tipsy.

'Normal, Nikolai Ivanovich', he said. 'What is it you say in English? Without news is good news. Only, I cannot find our neighbour Konstantin Andreyevich.'

'What a pity,' I said. 'I'm sorry.'

'My friend Konstantin Andreyevich,' he went on. 'He lives in the building behind the church. He isn't answering his phone.' He peered at me as if maybe I might say, *Oh that Konstantin Andreyevich, you should have said, he's upstairs in my kitchen.*

Instead I just tried to smile and look pained at the same time. 'I am sure everything is okay,' I said. I remember thinking that Konstantin Andreyevich, whoever he was, had probably had his phone disconnected or drunk himself into temporary deafness. But I did my best to take Oleg Nikolaevich seriously.

'Maybe he has gone to his brother in Tver.'

'Maybe,' I said.

'Perhaps,' he said, 'you can help me. Help me to find him.'

'I would be happy to,' I said. 'But I'm not sure there's anything I can do.'

'Yes, you can,' he said. 'You are a lawyer. An American.'

'I'm not American.'

'Well,' he insisted, 'you have a credit card. You have a secretary. You can speak to the police or to the prosecutor's office. I am an old man. This is Russia.'

'Okay,' I said. 'Of course. If I can help you, I will. I will try. I promise, Oleg Nikolaevich.'

He came towards me, and for a second I thought he was going to grab me or punch me. But instead he put his hand on my left shoulder, and his mouth very close to my right ear, so that when he spoke his tongue was virtually in it.

'Respected Nikolai Ivanovich,' he said, 'only an idiot smiles all the time.'

| FIVE

I guess there might in theory have been a time, maybe in the early afternoons, when Steve Walsh got by for more than five minutes without either a shot of coffee or a slug of red wine – just as in theory there must be a short, intermediary thirty-something phase in the lives of Russian women between high-heeled exhibitionism and middle-aged spread. But whenever I saw Steve he was chugging down one or other of his drugs. Like most of the expat alcoholics he had a tactic for persuading himself that he wasn't one: he ordered his wine by the glass, even if he drank twelve or twenty of them at a sitting, which was worse for his wallet but better for his self-esteem. When I saw him for lunch and told him about Masha and me, he had already graduated from coffee to vino.

'So,' Steve said, after I summarized the relationship so far, 'has she got you to buy her anything yet? Diamonds? Car? Tit job maybe?'

'It isn't like that.'

'What is it like?'

'It's different, Steve. Don't.'

'Do you think she wants you for your looks?'

Steve was technically British, but he had been trying to avoid England and himself for so long and in so many far-out places – Mexico for three or four years before Moscow, I think, and before that the Balkans, and before that somewhere else that I and maybe even he can't remember – that by the time I met him he had become one of those lost foreign correspondents that you read about in Graham Greene, a citizen of the republic of cynicism. He exploited me for leads I wasn't supposed to give him – hints about which cartel was borrowing how much from who, to take over which oil or aluminium firm, equations of greed that helped him to work out who was up and who was down in the Kremlin, who was going to be the next President and who was heading for a prison camp in Magadan. Steve pretended to check my leads, then used them in his articles for the *Independent* and some Canadian paper that his London employers didn't know about. I exploited him too, for conversation in English that wasn't about bonuses. We exploited each other. In other words, we were friends. I think maybe he was my only real friend in Moscow.

He was slimy blond and must once have been handsome, but by then he was furrowed and rioja florid. He looked a bit like Boris Yeltsin.

'Steve,' I said, 'don't take the piss, but I think I might be in love.'

You've never been the jealous type, though on the other hand you've never had much to be jealous of. My guess is you can live with this.

'Fucking Christ,' Steve said, waving his glass in the air.

We were eating beef stroganoff in the French restaurant at the back of the Smolensky shopping centre, where the mistresses of minigarchs go to drink overpriced tea between pedicures. It was, I think, almost the end of November. The big, heavy snow had just arrived, falling overnight like a practical joke, making a new city in an hour. Ugly things became beautiful, beautiful things became magical. Red Square was an instant film set – the encrusted mausoleum and snow-dusted Kremlin on one side, and the imperial department store lit up like a fairground on the other. On building sites and in churchyards, packs of stray dogs were optimistically nosing around in the mush. The street taxis had hiked their prices: you could tell how long foreigners had been in Moscow by the length of time they would stand in the whiteness negotiating. The begging babushkas had assumed their blackmailing winter position, kneeling in the pavement snow with their arms outstretched. And beneath the fur coats and grimaces, you knew that the Russians were happy, relatively speaking. Because, along with the fatalism and the borsch, the snow is part of what makes them them and nobody else.

'She loves me too, I think. Or she could. She likes me at least.'

'Did she tell you that?'

'No.'

'Listen,' he said, 'if she does, she'll mean it. She'll mean it at the moment she says it. But twenty minutes later she'll mean it when she nicks your credit card. They mean everything.'

'Have you ever been in love, Steve?'

'You know what you need, Nick? You need to lose your moral bearings. Otherwise you're done for.'

I changed the subject. I'd decided to ask Steve if he could help me to help my neighbour Oleg Nikolaevich find his friend. I'd been to the police myself, as I said I would, but I hadn't got anywhere. Masha had come with me: at the last minute Oleg Nikolaevich himself said he had an urgent appointment and couldn't go, though I think he may just have been put off by an ingrained fear of uniforms. The pimply adolescent detective we saw was wearing jeans and listening to gangsta rap. Above his desk he had a sign that said, 'I cannot drink flowers or chocolates', plus black and white portraits of Russia's weasel President and Erwin Rommel. He'd given us the special look that, like their womenfolk, some Russian men have – a commercial version of a pass, a sort of cash-hither smile. 'You need to pay,' Masha whispered to me in English. I refused, and the detective told me there was no evidence of a crime and therefore there was nothing he could do. As we were leaving he said that if ever I was in a hurry to get to a meeting or the airport he could loan me a couple of motorcycle outriders. ('Well,' said Oleg Nikolaevich when I told him what had happened at the police station, 'as long as we are alive, it is possible that one day we will be happy.')

I thought maybe Steve might know a friendly policeman, or a tame spook, or a housebreaker, someone who might be able to make some enquiries, jog a few memories or consciences.

Steve said he was sorry, but the policemen he knew weren't that sort of policeman. He told me not to waste my time, because Konstantin Andreyevich was probably dead – fallen into the river or under a car, or maybe he had drunk the wrong moonshine and keeled over in a forest.

'Don't get too attached,' Steve said. 'They only live to sixty. Stay here long enough and people you know are gonna die. You know two Russians over sixty, chances are one of them's gonna snuff it. Especially the men. They drink themselves into the ground before they get to see their pensions. You're bored in the Metro, there's a game you can play: try to spot an old man. Russian I-Spy.'

'Any other ideas, Steve? I mean, to help find him. Seriously. He's a nice old geezer, my neighbour. But no money or *krisha* or anything. I think I'm his best hope.'

'This is Russia,' said Steve. 'Pray.'

I gave up and asked him whether he knew anything about my new business acquaintance, the Cossack. He found the Cossack much more interesting.

'Little guy?' said Steve. 'Pale, slimy eyes?'

Yes, I said. That was him.

'He's not an oil man,' Steve said. 'He works for the FSB.' In case you don't recognize the initials, the FSB is the new-model KGB, minus the communism and the rules. 'The story goes that he was done for murder, somewhere in the Urals in the early nineties. The FSB signed him up in prison, got him out and sent him over to the Far East to help with their poaching scams. I've never actually met him but I was in a bar on Sakhalin Island once and a Scottish helicopter pilot pointed him out to me. He'd been up in Kamchatka running the caviar racket, I think the pilot said, until they'd moved him on to salmon. He was being lined up for deputy governor of the island, but then they shipped him out. I haven't heard of him since. I guess he did so well in fish that they promoted him to the oil team. Crime, business, politics, spookery – the usual Russian merry-go-round.'

'Maybe he quit the FSB and went into business,' I said.

'They're all in business,' Steve said, 'but they never quit. There are no ex-KGB men, just like the President says.'

I asked him whether he knew anything about the oil terminal scheme in the north that our loan was financing. The deal seemed to be going smoothly: the Cossack was on course to get the first tranche of his money soon. The banks that were lending it to him had cash-flow models and feasibility studies for the project, drawn up by the usual swarm of consultants, and a hundred pages of waivers and indemnities drawn up by us. As a matter of form we were seeking guarantees of cooperation from the governor of the region where the terminal was being built, from Narodneft about the amount of oil they'd pump through it after it was constructed, and from the Cossack about the revenue that would be set aside for repayments in an escrow account. All of these were on their way, we were assured. Everything was on track on the site, the Cossack told us: he was sure that the terminal would be pumping its first oil cargoes into the tankers that would dock with it by the end of the following summer. The only glitch was that when Vyacheslav Alexandrovich the surveyor had been getting ready to visit, the Cossack's people said there had been a small fire and that he'd better hang on for a few weeks.

'Sounds plausible,' Steve said. 'The Russians have more or less run out of pipeline capacity, so they're desperate for new export routes. The President was on about it in his last television phone-in: "This is one of the great challenges for Russia's economy, we welcome help and investment from our foreign partners," the usual claptrap. And sea-borne oil is supposed to be the next big thing. Gets it out to the European market without relying on the bolshy neighbours who the Russkis keep falling out with. They've got an ice-free bay up there somewhere – I think it's on the Gulf Stream – that must be what they're using. Who are the partners?'

It was just the logistics firm and Narodneft, I said.

'Interesting. Listen, I'm sure your banks will be okay. The Russians have got the oil and they need to sell it. They know the rules: they can keep ripping their own people off, so long as they play nice with the foreigners. But there's always an angle in it for them somewhere, Nick. I'm guessing they'll use the logistics outfit to cream off some of the takings, when they start making money, so Narodneft doesn't have to share it all with the public. You know what Narodneft means?'

'Yes.'

'"People's oil". Fucking joke.'

Steve had once been summoned to the Ministry of Foreign Affairs to be screamed at for going down to Chechnya without permission, then writing up the chats he'd had with self-confessed Russian war criminals for his newspapers. The ministry had threatened to revoke his visa, and in reply, so legend had it, he'd told them to go ahead, throw him out, make his day. If that really happened, he'd been bluffing, because like all the journalists I ever met in Moscow, Steve loved Russia. It had all the plush restaurants and imported beer that they could wish for, but it had preserved enough old-school bad habits to keep the hacks in column inches and on the other side of the world from whatever it was they were running away from. Most of them, Steve especially, disguised their love with a sort of moral machismo. It was as if he had a contractual obligation to see the worst in everyone and every-thing, or pretend to. For a degenerate he could sometimes be a real pious asshole.

'I don't know, Steve,' I said. 'It's standard practice for oil majors, you know that: they set up a separate company for new investments to keep the debts off the balance sheet. It isn't just Narodneft, the big western firms do it too.' That was true, it was a normal accounting manoeuvre. Though probably I only tried to defend the Cossack because Steve had needled me over me and Masha.

'It's not a western firm, Nick. Listen,' he said, swigging, 'you have to understand, the Soviet Union produced the opposite of what it was meant to. They were all supposed to love each other, but it ended with no one giving a shit about anyone else. Not the public. Not shareholders. Not even you.'

I knew where his spiel went from there: communism didn't ruin Russia, it was the other way round, and after three more glasses, the rise of the KGB state, the legacy of Ivan the Terrible and the comparative advantages of women from St Petersburg. Looking at his dead flecked eyes, I decided that Steve was jealous – of me and Masha, of anyone who had the hope and the ambition to be happy. His meandering Russian history lecture was just getting on to the long-term impact of the Mongol yoke when I interrupted him.

'I feel like shit,' I said, lying as I pushed away my plate. 'Big night with Masha last night. I think I should go. Sorry, Steve. Let's do it again soon, okay?'

'We all feel like shit,' said Steve, raising an eyebrow at a waiter and tapping his glass. 'It's fucking Russia. The booze. The pollution. The shit food. The fucking airplanes. The crap that falls out of the sky when it rains, you don't even want to think about. Russia is like polonium. It attacks all your organs at once.'

'What are you working on now?' I asked him as I put on my scarf.

'Big energy story,' he said. 'Much bigger than your little oil terminal.'

'What's the angle this time? Business or politics?'

'In Russia,' Steve said, 'there are no business stories. And there are no politics stories. There are no love stories. There are only crime stories.'

| SIX

There were times in every Russian winter when I thought I might not make it. Times when I might have headed straight for the airport, if I hadn't known the traffic would be so terrible. Walking became an obstacle course, with mounds of snow to swerve around and narrow runs of passable pavement that you battled over with people coming the other way. You know that thing that happens in London, when you run into someone on the pavement, and when you try to get around them they move in the same direction as you, and you're still in each other's way – but in the end you work it out, smile at the accidental intimacy and harmless bad luck and carry on? That doesn't happen in Moscow. Once a month or so I forgot to curl my toes inside my fur-lined boots, my feet went cycling upwards, my arse downwards, and I lived through a long, long second of flailing helpless terror as I waited to hit the ice.

Then there are the orange men. Every year, after the first proper snowfall, someone in the mayor's office pushes a button, and an army of men in orange overalls, new-age serfs from Tajikistan, Uzbekistan and Whereverstan, emerge like placid invading aliens from under the earth or the other side of the city's outer ring road. They drive around in prehistoric trucks, shovelling snow into piles and taking out stubborn patches of ice with WMD-grade chemicals. In the street where I lived they piled all the snow on one side, burying any cars that had been carelessly left there, which that winter included the rusting Zhiguli. And every night, at about four in the morning, the orange men come with shovels to hack the ice off the pavements, making a noise that only the dead could sleep through – a noise somewhere between the screech of fingernails on glass, the banging of a shipyard and the yowling of randy cats. The worst part was my own bastard ingratitude. I resented them, but at the same time I knew it was only stupid chance that meant I was warm and inside, sometimes with a woman beside me, while they were outside breaking their backs.

One grumpy evening, around the end of November, instead of running to the airport I fled to Masha and the mobile phone shop where she worked, down near Novokuznetskaya Metro station. She wasn't expecting me. I turned right up towards the Tretyakov Gallery, past a derelict church and opposite it a subterranean café I'd been to once, where privileged Russian kids listen to angry music and pretend to be dissidents. Just after that was Masha's shop. I peered in through the window.

She was sitting behind a desk with her hair in an Alice band, listening as a stone-washed young couple explained their telephonic needs. The shop had a reception area where you took a numbered ticket from a machine, and waited to be called into the office where Masha and the other sales staff sat. It was standing-room-only pandemonium, the atmosphere like I imagine the inside of the Ark. (There were more mobile phones than people in Moscow then, largely, it was said, because of all the men who had a separate number for speaking to their mistresses.) A woman in the far corner was whining as if she was giving birth. I wiped my steamed-up glasses and was elbowing my way through the crowd when the inner doors opened and Masha came out to meet me.

'Kolya,' she said in her amazing growl, that voice that reached into my insides, 'go please to Raskolnikov's on Pyatnitskaya and wait. I will be twenty minutes maybe.'

'Okay,' I said. I watched as she walked back to her desk, her lower half encased in tight black office-girl trousers, her upper curves softened by a racing-green company sweatshirt.

I did as I was told and waited by the window in Raskolnikov's, a warm café that was buried in a little courtyard and not trying too hard to be found. Eventually Masha turned into the courtyard. She was wearing a coat that resembled a sort of red patchwork duvet, only sexier. She had three-inch heels that she'd put on after her shift, on which she somehow walked through the snow like Jesus on water. She had perfect winter suspension. She came in, took off her coat and sat down opposite me.

'How was work?' I said.

'What is problem with you?'

I don't know what I'm doing here, I wanted to say, a*nd not just in Russia either, I'm lonely, I love you.*

I didn't say that, you won't be surprised to hear. I mumbled something English instead. I said I was feeling a bit low, a bit tired, that I wanted to see her, that I hoped she didn't mind the intrusion.

'Listen,' she said. 'On Saturday we go to dacha.'

'What dacha?'

The Russian dacha is a physical place, the most physical place, the earthy retreat where you grow potatoes, pickle onions and go fishing. But it's also a place in the imagination, the place that is not Moscow, where there are no traffic jams, no hustlers and no police.

'It is dacha of my friend Anya's grandfather. But he is never going there. There is *banya,* we will make shashlik. With Katya. You will feel better.'

'Okay,' I said. 'Good.'

'But first in morning we go to Butovo.'

'Why will we go to Butovo?'

'We go with Tatiana Vladimirovna,' Masha said.

'Why is Tatiana Vladimirovna going to Butovo?'

Butovo is a suburb that clings to the monstrous city at its far southern rim, the kind of place that I guess used to be a separate village before Moscow bloated out to engulf it, like the ones in Middlesex sucked into London by the Tube.

'She maybe wants to live there, and on Saturday we go with her so she may decide.'

I remembered them referring to their scheme, that afternoon when Masha and Katya introduced me to their aunt. I figured this must have been it.

Masha put her hand under the table and on to my knee, sliding her nails up the inside of my thigh. 'Don't worry, Kolya,' she said. 'I love you.'

* * *

On the Saturday the three of us buzzed the crackly intercom outside Tatiana Vladimirovna's building and asked her if she was ready. 'Always ready,' she said, letting us in so we didn't have to wait outside in the slush. 'Always ready' was the slogan of the Pioneers, Masha told me – the old Soviet equivalent of the Scouts, who were taught how to unmask spies and denounce kulaks as well as to build campfires.

Tatiana Vladimirovna came down to meet us wearing a kind of reinforced winter tunic, brown and padded, a bright blue scarf, mittens and what in Luton in the eighties were called moon boots. She was carrying a big plastic bag, inside which, it turned out, there was a Tupperware box of pickled herrings, some hardboiled eggs and a flask of sweet tea, which she began to press on us as soon as we'd changed Metro lines at Borovitskaya and settled in for the long ride out to Butovo. She'd wrapped up some salt in a piece of brown paper for us to put on the eggs.

'A long time ago,' Tatiana Vladimirovna whispered to me in Russian, 'Pyotr Arkadyevich and I used to go out to Butovo to pick mushrooms in the forest and swim in the pond. But there was no Metro then. We took a bus and then we walked.'

We were going back there, Masha explained to me, because Tatiana Vladimirovna knew a man called Stepan Mikhailovich whose company was building a new block of flats on the very edge of town, and Tatiana Vladimirovna was thinking about moving into it. She was going to stop working at her museum in the spring, Masha said, and wanted to get out of the centre of Moscow, where there were too many cars and criminals and not enough forest. The plan was that she would swap her place by the pond for the one in Butovo.

It was a legacy of Soviet times, Masha told me, the idea of swapping apartments. You never owned your flat in the old days, she said – you never owned anything, except maybe your grave – but you could swap your right to live in it for someone else's right to live somewhere else. Some people still went in for swaps, Masha said, partly because they didn't trust themselves not to drink the proceeds if they got paid in cash for their properties. In this case, she said, Stepan Mikhailovich would probably give Tatiana Vladimirovna some money as well, because her flat in the centre was worth more than the new one in Butovo. They hadn't agreed how much he would give her, they'd discuss the details later. That day we were going to meet him and look at the flat, then come back to Moscow, pick up supplies and take another train out to the dacha.

* * *

The old part of the Moscow Metro, in the city centre, is the sort of subway system you get if you give a tyrannical maniac all the marble, onyx and disposable human beings he can dream of. But the network gives up on its malachite and stained glass and fancy bas reliefs, and pushes up above ground, long before it gets out to Butovo, which is about as far as it goes. When we came out of the Metro station there were new high-rise apartment buildings all around, white and peach and not as ugly as the Soviet ones, with stubbly patches of lawn between them.

We flagged down a car, and on the way to the building, I remember, the driver gave us a rapid-fire lament for his lost youth and lost motherland. He was an engineer in Soviet times, he told us. 'These days,' he said, 'the Chinese are too cunning for us…We are giving away all our natural resources…everyone over forty is finished in Russia.' We drove out towards where the high-rises stopped and turned left.

The building we arrived at marked the end of Moscow. On one side was all city and stress, but on the other side of the road was the sort of Butovo that Tatiana Vladimirovna remembered from many years before, a wonky Russian idyll of sloping wooden houses and little orchards alongside and behind them. Beyond the houses, with their ornamental window frames, rickety fences and rusty roofs, was a grove of silver birch trees, and beyond that a greener forest – a forest that looked like you could still hunt for mushrooms there.

It was about ten thirty or eleven in the morning. We stood outside the building's entrance, stamping our feet and waiting for Stepan Mikhailovich to arrive. It was cold, but I'd graduated to my ultimate winter coat, a black Michelin-man ski number with a thermonuclear lining, which kept my blood flowing even down at Napoleonic temperatures. The air was less acrid than in the city centre. We could taste the pine trees.

Masha made a phone call. Then she said, 'He is coming, Stepan Mikhailovich is coming.'

Stepan Mikhailovich arrived after about five minutes. He was a thin man with a little ponytail and a nervous smile. He can't have been over twenty-five, but since lots of high-flying Russian businessmen were virtually pubescent I wasn't too surprised. He shook hands with Masha, Katya and me and bowed to Tatiana Vladimirovna. We went inside, Stepan Mikhailovich last, groping for a light switch. The building wasn't finished: the walls were unpainted, the floor in the vestibule was uncovered and the heating didn't seem to work. It was at least as cold as it was in the street. The lift hadn't been installed yet, so we walked up the concrete steps to the seventh floor and the apartment that might soon be Tatiana Vladimirovna's, brushing aside rogue electrical wires that had escaped from their brackets on the ceiling. Tatiana Vladimirovna wouldn't take the arm I offered her, but stopped twice to bend over, gasp, and clutch her knees. The building smelled of paint and glue.

On the seventh floor Stepan Mikhailovich opened the stubborn door to an apartment with a key and his shoulder. The apartment wasn't ready either, everything was bare and plaster-coloured, but you could see how it was supposed to be: a little Ikean paradise, with big windows and high-ish ceilings, two large boxy bedrooms and a kitchen built into the living room. There were two balconies, one looking back towards Moscow from a bedroom and the other, off the living room, facing the forest.

'You see, Tatiana Vladimirovna,' said Masha as we stood in the living room, 'you will no longer have to carry your food through from the kitchen like you have to now.'

Tatiana Vladimirovna didn't answer but went out on to the balcony. I followed her, making sure I'd be able to spring back inside if it collapsed. From above you could see the chaos of entangled plots on the other side of the road, and a couple of tough tethered goats, and the glint of a frozen pond somewhere in the trees. Above them the sun was shining vaguely through the milky November sky, old but strong. In April – between the thaw and the jungly green explosion of the summer – or in raw mid-October, I bet the same view would have been barren and depressing. But when we stood there all the bits of old tractors and discarded refrigerators, the shoals of empty vodka bottles and dead animals that tend to litter the Russian countryside were invisible, smothered by the annual oblivion of the snow. The snow let you forget the scars and blemishes, like temporary amnesia for a bad conscience.

Tatiana Vladimirovna breathed in deeply, and sighed. I thought I could see her anticipating the rest of her life, a lucky unexpected coda spent making the gooey fruit compotes that old Russian women like to ferment, talking to other babushkas in their headscarves, pretending the last seventy years had never happened.

'Do you like it, Tatiana Vladimirovna?' Masha called out.

Again Tatiana Vladimirovna didn't answer but came back inside and walked around the living room. She paused by a window at the side of the building that took in both the end of the town and the beginning of the countryside. Through it you could see the white towers of a church hunkering in the forest, with little gold domes and silver Orthodox crosses riding on top of them.

'I think,' said Tatiana Vladimirovna, 'that this is where I will put Pyotr Arkadyevich's desk. What do you think, Nikolai?'

'I think that would be very nice,' I said. I did truly think it was nice and right for her, I'm sure I did. But I didn't think enough. I wanted to get back to the city and out to the dacha, and the *banya*, and the night.

'Yes,' Katya said, smiling her inscrutable smile, her sweet nose pink from the chill, 'it is very pleasant, Tatiana Vladimirovna. Very beautiful. And such fresh air!'

'Stepan Mikhailovich,' said Masha, pacing up to him over the cold floor in her red duvet coat and touching him on the arm, 'when do you think this building will be ready?'

'I think in a month,' said Stepan Mikhailovich. A month seemed optimistic, though in Russia you never knew. They could wallow in mud and vodka for a decade, then conjure up a skyscraper or execute a royal family in an afternoon, if they put their minds to it and the incentives were right.

Stepan Mikhailovich paused and then said, 'I think Tatiana Vladimirovna will be very happy here. It is clean, and there are not too many cars or immigrants.'

Tatiana Vladimirovna smiled and went out on to the balcony again, alone. I saw her lift a gloved hand to her eyes. I thought she might be crying, but I was standing behind her and I couldn't say for sure.

I hadn't done anything to be ashamed of, had I? Anything you could hold against me? Not really. Not yet.

* * *

We offered to walk Tatiana Vladimirovna home but she waved us away. Instead we said goodbye and left her on the Metro when we got off to change on to the red line for the two stops to Pushkinskaya. We walked down Bolshaya Bronnaya to the supermarket around the corner from my building. At the butcher's counter I made another hand gesture that, like the flick of the neck and the tap of invisible epaulettes that Masha had taught me that evening in Dream of the East, seemed to be understood by every Russian. I held out my hands in front of me and twisted my wrists, as if I was twirling two imaginary knobs. The man behind the counter understood the sign for shashlik, and wrapped up a kilo of marinated lamb. We caught a commuter train from frilly Belorussky station, out of the other end of the city from Butovo and towards the promised dacha.

For an hour on the rattling train, I remember, the three of us were jostled by a kind of shabby cabaret – a chain of beggars and hawkers chasing each other through the carriages, selling beer, pens, cigarettes, roasted sunflower seeds, bootleg DVDs, all-purpose perfume (for wearing or drinking). Or they were playing the accordion, or explaining how they'd lost a leg or a husband in Chechnya. There were prostitutes, runaways, assorted human sacrifices. I gave a hundred roubles to an old woman with a lopsided face and a thin coat. At about three o'clock, I think, we got off.

Already it was beautiful. The station was just a single wooden platform on stilts, with an old-fashioned sign that said 'Orekhovo' or 'Polinkovo' or something, one of the cutesy pre-revolutionary Russian country names that got changed when they collectivized everything, then brought back again after the wall came down. We stood alone on the platform, mingling our breaths and cutting deep shadows into the snow. There was forest all around us, the branches of the trees covered in snow like they'd been outlined in icing sugar. We shuffled along to the steps at the end of the platform, and crossed over the rails and the wooden slats between them, Masha and Katya attached to my elbows. We went up a vague path through a clump of silver birches, their branches too cunningly angular for the snow to have really settled on, in the direction of what looked like human activity.

It's a strange country, Russia, with its talented sinners and occasional saint, bona fide saints that only a place of such accomplished cruelty could produce, a crazy mix of filth and glory. It was the same combination that afternoon. It turned out to be the sort of Russian village where it looks like a war's just ended, even though it hasn't: the kind that anybody sober and able-bodied has fled, leaving behind only the lunatics, criminals and policemen. There was one shop. A pair of ruined bearded men stood outside, possibly waiting for a third to turn up and share a bottle of vodka with them. We went in to buy drinking water and charcoal.

The girls took the bags from Moscow and the charcoal, leaving me with just the water, the handles of the big plastic containers biting through my winter gloves. They steered me down a track that ran alongside a grey block of flats and led to a rusty little gate. Masha opened it with a big old key like a prison warden's, and we were back in Christmas-card Russia, the birches alternating with still lush pines, the ground between them a naïvely pure white. As we waded through the snow the odd twig snapped with a sound like a cracked whip, which ricocheted off the trees around us. A hundred metres in there was a half-frozen stream, rivulets racing between the mating slabs of ice, which we crossed on a stringy footbridge with missing boards and a fairground swing. I felt as if I was an extra in a Siberian *Indiana Jones*.

On the other side of the stream, spaced out between the trees, were the dachas – ramshackle wooden cottages poking out of the snow. I saw smoke coming from one of the chimneys but the rest seemed deserted. Icicles like ornate daggers descended from the overhanging roofs. We didn't see any other people.

Our place was about the fifth or sixth cottage along, set in a submerged garden, the snow disturbed only by the shallow geometric patterns left by birds' feet. The building leaned at an ominous Pisan angle, and looked from the outside like one of those slapstick houses in a silent film, as if it was poised to collapse and leave us standing in a window frame amid the harmless wreckage. But inside it was much more spacious than seemed feasible. In the front room there was a stopped grandfather clock, photographs of dead ancestors in smudgy frames and a bare electric bulb hanging from the ceiling. There was a sofa that must once have been someone's treasure, with patched gold fabric and a motif of nustling storks carved into the panels below the armrests. In a small second room we found a gas ring and a canister, a table, and an unexpected staircase that led to a bedroom in the eaves. The bedroom had a made-up single bed and a frosted window that looked out into the forest.

Masha was immediately on her knees, stuffing lumps of wood from a basket by the door into the mouth of a stove – an old Russian stove that was built into the wall, the sort that the house serfs used to sleep on top of. Katya went out to start cooking the *banya*, a separate little hut with its own stove and chimney about twenty metres beyond the dacha, almost in the trees. Masha pointed out the barbecue, a functional tub of metal with detachable legs that was hiding under a table.

I unwrapped the meat we'd bought in Moscow and slid the chunks on to impressively crusty skewers. I went outside with the barbecue and the charcoal. I stood on my own, tending the fire in the winter silence. It started to snow again, the wide weightless flakes sizzling on the coals. Standing there, I remember, I experienced the blissful sense of well-being that expats sometimes enjoy. I was a long way from things and people that I didn't want to think about – including myself, my old self, the so-what lawyer with the so-what life I'd left behind in London. The me that you know now. I was in a place where today, every day, almost anything might happen.

An hour or so later we were sitting abreast on the sofa in the warmed-up dacha, eating barbecued lamb with flat Armenian bread and a hot Georgian pomegranate sauce, drinking snow-chilled vodka from chipped shot glasses, chased down with beer. Masha's hair was down over her shoulders. They both ate with the quiet intent opportunism that Russians seem to inherit.

'I like your friend,' Katya said.

'What friend?'

'At club. At Rasputin. Friend who help us.'

'He's not my friend,' I said.

'Maybe he should be your friend,' Masha said. 'He is useful person.'

She smiled, though I don't think she was joking. I liked her frankness. But I didn't want to talk about the Cossack.

'Who is Anya?' I asked them.

'Who?' said Katya.

'The girl whose grandfather owns this dacha.'

'Her grandfather has dacha from time he work for railway,'

Katya explained. 'Railway owned all this land and gave everybody piece. But he never come and Anya live now in Nizhny Novgorod. I think maybe grandfather is dead. She also is our sister.'

'You have another sister?'

They smiled. They thought about it.

'You know, Kolya,' said Masha, 'in Russian this word sister means not only daughter of your parents. It also can mean daughter of parents' brother or sister. I think in English you have one other word for sister of this type?'

'Cousin,' I said. 'I didn't know that.'

'*Da,*' Masha said. 'Cousin.'

'And what kind of sister is Katya?' I asked.

'She is also cousin,' said Masha, after a pause.

'Yes,' said Katya, her cheeks flushed from the sauce and the vodka, 'I am cousin.' She licked up the last traces from her hands.

'Are your family also in Murmansk? With Masha's mother?'

'I think yes,' Katya said. 'Yes, in Murmansk.'

Not sisters, then. Not quite everything I thought they were. For the first time, with them, I felt like I sometimes did when it dawned on me that a Moscow taxi driver was drunk or mad, and I sat fingering the door handle in the back of his car and contemplating when to leap out, all the time knowing that in fact I wouldn't. I never did.

I might have asked more about their family, and how they were all related, but Masha put down her plate and said, 'Let's go, *banya* is ready.'

* * *

The outhouse had a tiny greasy anteroom, about the size of a large wardrobe, with a couple of hooks on the wall and a hatch for the stove into which Katya fed a couple more logs. We stood there for a few seconds, like we were strangers thrust together in a refrigerated lift. Then we took off our clothes, arses and elbows bumping and rubbing. They were both wearing G-strings – my impression is that unmarried Russian women are obliged to wear them by law – frilly pink for Katya with a matching bra, I can't remember Masha's. They took those off too. I pulled off the posh boxer shorts I'd chosen with such care, and put my glasses into one of my winter boots. 'Okay,' Masha said, 'hurry!' and we darted into the heat before it could escape.

It had none of the amenities – the lemon tea, the savage masseurs, the hushed conversation of powerful hairy men – that you get in the upscale Moscow places I sometimes went to with Paolo. But this is definitely the *banya* that I remember best. There was a rough home-made bench, and one window that let in the fading light from outside. In the wall opposite the window was a metal plate that formed the back of the stove: to make steam you threw water from a little bucket against the metal. It was already impossibly hot. We sat down on the bench, trying to keep our feet off the roasting floor. I was in the hottest seat, nearest to the stove, Katya was in the half-lit spot by the window. It was one of those situations when you try not to look, and fail, and console yourself that probably you were supposed to. She had mannequin-firm breasts, bigger than Masha's, and she wasn't a real blonde.

We sat skin to skin, our sweat running together and pooling on the floor.

'So, Kolya,' said Katya, 'what do you think from Butovo? As home for Tatiana Vladimirovna.'

'I thought it was very nice.'

'I am not sure,' said Masha, her long legs just visible but her face in the dark. 'It is far away. Maybe I like old apartment of Tatiana Vladimirovna more.'

'But if she want to go to Butovo,' said Katya, 'maybe you help her, Kolya. I mean papers. Legal things. Papers for old apartment that Stepan Mikhailovich may need. She is old Soviet woman and does not understand.'

It was hard to talk, the hot air rushing in and scalding the back of my throat when I opened my mouth, and I just said, 'Yes.'

We baked for maybe twenty minutes. I was already dizzy

from the vodka and wanted to leave after about five, but I didn't want to be the first to quit. Finally Masha said, 'Now we wash.'

'How do we wash?'

'In snow,' said Katya.

'We jump in snow,' said Masha.

'Isn't that dangerous? You know,' I gasped, gesturing at my chest in the murk, 'for the heart.'

'Life is dangerous,' said Masha, dripping an arm around me. 'No one survived it yet.'

We slipped out on the sweaty floor and closed the door. We went straight through the anteroom. Masha and Katya dived giggling and face down into a patch of deep untouched snow by the back fence, under a heavy pine tree. I shivered for about three seconds and jumped after them.

It felt as if I'd been slapped all over, or stung by a thousand bees, but in a good way, the snow killing the heat of the *banya* in an arrested heartbeat. More than that, it felt as if I'd done something reckless, like a high dive or a train robbery, and lived through it. The tingly pain proved that I was alive, every inch of me was alive, more alive than ever.

That's the truth about the Russians that I missed until it was too late. The Russians will do the impossible thing: the thing you think they can't do, the thing you haven't even thought of. They will set fire to Moscow when the French are coming or poison each other in foreign cities. They will do it, and afterwards they will behave as if nothing has happened at all. And if you stay in Russia long enough, so will you.

When we stood up I looked down into the snow, now dull but luminous in the darkness, and to my weak glasses-less eyes the hollow that Masha's body had made looked like the shape of an angel. We ran back into the outhouse, our feet numbing, ice forming in our hair. Katya snatched up her stuff and ran out naked again up to the dacha. I picked up my boots, but Masha took them from me, dropped them, and led me back into the heat.

'Did you have a *banya* in Murmansk?' I asked her. I could barely see her any more through the scorching gloom.

'Yes,' she said, and that was all she said.

She felt strange at first, cold like a corpse from the snow almost everywhere except her mouth, but wet and electric. She was my private oblivion, my personal avalanche in the thin air of the *banya*. She blotted out, for those minutes, the creepy Cossack, the waste of my thirties and all my doubts.

* * *

I woke up during the night with absolutely no idea where I was. I remember calming myself with the thought that I was in my bed in Birmingham, in the last student house I lived in, on one of the rougher streets in Edgbaston. Then I saw Masha asleep alongside me, underneath the worn covers in the narrow attic bed. The fine blond hairs on the knots of her spine glowed in the moonlight from the window, like a love letter written on her body in invisible ink.

I needed to piss, the nocturnal weakness that ambushed me in my mid-thirties – an early signpost to the grave, if you stop to think about it, like the new and upsetting head-crushing hangovers of your twenties. I creaked down the stairs in my boxer shorts, passed Katya sleeping on the sofa, put on my boots and coat and waddled outside. I pissed, and saw the animal warmth of myself melting the deep snow in front of me. By the moonlight I could make out the submerged green leaves at the bottom of the hole I had cut in the whiteness.

When I think back now, writing this, about my lost years in Moscow, despite everything that happened and everything I did, I still look back on that night as my happiest time, the time I would always go back to if I could.

| SEVEN

Now and again, when I was in Moscow, I would hear in the street or through a window – or think I'd hear – a sound like the distinctive screech London black cabs make when they brake for a speed bump or to go round a corner. Now and again I would have liked someone to apologize to me when I stepped on their foot in the Metro, like people do on the Tube. On the basis of those reflexes I guess you might say that part of me missed England. I did sometimes wish I could decompress, just for an hour or so, in its law-abiding, unhectic familiarity. But the feeling was never enough for me to want to move back, not even at the end. London and Luton weren't really home any more.

On Christmas Eve that winter I was driven out to Domodedovo airport, through the grey slush, by a driver keen to share his scientific proof that Russian women were the best-looking in the world, with the possible exception of Venezuelans. The theory, I remember, had something to do with how few men there had been left in Russia after the war, and how they'd had their pick of the abundant girls, who in turn had given birth to beautiful daughters, and so on. Someone important must have been on the move because the streets were temporarily barricaded by police cars, and we got stuck beneath the snowy outstretched arm of the Lenin statue at Oktyabrskaya. The ice on the reservoir was blotchy with fishermen sitting next to the holes they had cut in it. At the airport, as my passport was stamped, I felt the lightness everyone always feels, even if they love Moscow – the lifting of the weight of rude shopkeepers and predatory police and impossible weather, the lightness of leaving Russia.

When we reached London it was already dark. From the air, the lights flashing along the roads and down the river and blazing in the football stadiums seemed to be putting on their electric show just for me, in my honour, the conquering corporate-law hero.

Three hours later, in my parents' Luton semi, I was howling on the inside and knocking back my father's supermarket-brand Scotch. They always make an effort but you know what they're like – it somehow manages to be claustrophobic and lonely at the same time. I arrived before the others and slept in the bedroom I shared with my brother until he went to university. My mum said again that she wanted to visit me, she wanted to see St Petersburg, and how was the beginning of March? Cold, I told her, still very cold. My father's back was playing up, but he tried, I could see that, asking me how work was going and whether the Russian President was as bad as they said in the papers. I don't know why he always seemed so disappointed with me underneath. It might have been a moral thing, because I did a job that was more about money than making the world a better place. Or it might have been the opposite, and me and Moscow and the money I was earning reminded him of everything he'd never done and never would do himself.

On Christmas Day my brother came in from Reading with his wife and their children, William (the one who pinched your iPod at my dad's seventieth) and Thomas, and my sister came up from London, alone. We gave each other the usual, impersonally practical presents, socks and scarves and I-give-up John Lewis vouchers. I'd brought Russian dolls and furry hats for the kids and picked up the rest in duty free.

It could have been nice. There was no reason for it not to be nice. It was just that we'd gone separate ways and lost each other, leaving nothing much in common besides a couple of soft-focus anecdotes, featuring donkey rides and ice-cream overdoses, that you've heard a dozen times, plus some old irritations that flare up like a phantom itch when we get together. The children had once felt like a second chance, for my brother and me, at least, but they let us down. We ate the turkey and said how moist it was, and lit up the Christmas pudding for the boys, then moved to the chintz sofas in the lounge wearing lopsided paper hats, persevering in the sort of dutiful drinking more likely to result in murder than authentic merriment.

We had a lively exchange about the new parking restrictions in the town centre, and a ritual disagreement about whether we should watch the Queen's Christmas message, as my father always wanted to. When my phone rang it was like hearing the all-clear in a bomb shelter.

'How is England, Kolya?'

I felt giddy, elated, like I might be sick. 'Fine. Okay. How is Moscow?'

'Moscow is Moscow,' Masha said. 'Bad roads and many fools. I am missing you. When I am in shop I think about you. At night I also think about you, Kolya.'

'*Sekundochku*,' I said: 'Just a second' in Russian, a bit of automatic camouflage that was doubtless more incriminating than talking in English. I rushed out of the room as though I'd been called by a teenage girlfriend. I went into the kitchen, where my mother had pinned her offspring's phone numbers to the fridge with a magnet from Durham Cathedral. On the window sill was a Christmas television guide, in which she'd put tragic little asterisks next to the programmes she wanted to watch. I'd been sucked, as I always was, into the time warp of family, the instant rewind that takes you back to the roles you've grown out of.

'I'm thinking about you too,' I said. 'I've told my family about you, Masha.' The second bit wasn't true, I just thought it was something she'd like to hear. But the first part was. I was already thinking of her and me as real life, and the rest as somehow distant and less important. I wanted to tell her about whatever had happened to me, as if somehow without her knowing about it, it hadn't really happened. Do you know what I mean?

I asked her about Katya, and her mother in Murmansk, and about Tatiana Vladimirovna.

'Listen, Kolya,' she said, 'maybe you will bring something for Tatiana Vladimirovna, something for New Year. I think maybe she is not receiving so many presents.'

'Of course,' I said. 'Good idea. Definitely. What should I bring?'

'You think of something, Kolya. Something English.'

There was more, and most of it I've forgotten, but I can remember her saying, 'I see you soon, Kolya. I think about you. I love you.'

I went back to the lounge, and they all averted their eyes in an ostentatious show of indifference. I felt trapped like you do after you've eaten your airline meal, and getting the stewardess to take away your tray so you can escape seems the only thing in the world that matters. Underneath it all, I suppose, was the knowledge that I could have turned out the same way as my parents, and the fear that maybe I still could – that I might not manage to make my own life at all.

We sat looking at the children, willing them to do something adorable or eccentric. I lasted till the day after Boxing Day, then moved my return flight forward by a week to take me back home, back to Moscow, just before New Year.

* * *

I hurried through the scrum of lean Russian youths who were wrestling for their parents' luggage at the baggage carousels, and out into the crush of criminal-looking taxi drivers in the arrivals hall – into that particular Russian everyday war, the war of everyone against everyone else. I marched up through the check-in desks and bought a ticket for the train into the city.

The big freeze was on, the real cryogenic deal that I could

feel in my teeth, and then everywhere else, when I stepped out of the clammy underpass and into the fierce air at Pushkin Square, after the airport train and the Metro. It hadn't been that cold when I'd left for England, minus ten maybe. Walking down the Bulvar to my place, I remember, my breath froze differently from the way it had before Christmas, congealing into a kind of tangible fog. The bit of exposed skin on my cheeks, between my upturned collar and my pulled-down hat, stung and then went numb. My nostrils froze together, the hairs inside them hugging each other for survival. The electronic thermometer outside McDonald's said minus twenty-seven. It was so cold that there was almost nobody smoking in the streets. The traffic police had been issued with old-fashioned felt boots, an ancient Russian precaution that kept their feet from falling off while they hung around extorting bribes from people.

I called Masha and arranged to spend New Year's Eve with her and Katya and, at least to start with, Tatiana Vladimirovna. There were two days of work left before the statutory ten-day New Year break, a national binge referred to by my colleagues as the 'oligarch skiing holiday'. I had nothing else to do, so I went into the office on the day after I got back.

'That fucking surveyor,' Paolo said when I shut the door to his office. Beneath his window the orange men burrowing around in the white expanse of Paveletskaya Square looked like an army of angry ants. 'That fucking Cossack.'

'Happy New Year, Paolo.'

'It is almost finished,' he said. 'The client is almost happy. Everyone is almost happy. Except for this surveyor. Where is he, Nicholas?'

'I don't know.'

'You know, sometimes I wish we never saw the Cossack at all. Why must it be project finance? Why must it be the British Virgin Islands? Always the British Virgin Islands. How are you, by the way?'

| EIGHT

The truth is that, in those days, even the bankers didn't care all that much whether the banks they worked for got their money back. They earned their bonuses just for shelling it out, and would probably have moved on or upstairs before the Russians or whoever got a chance to default. All the western banks were desperate to do business in Moscow, because everyone else seemed to be, and most of them weren't too fussed about the destination of their loans. Half the time, when they were lending to one of the huge energy or metals firms, the bankers handed over the cash with no security at all: the Russians were drowning in petrodollars, and anyway the firms' bosses knew they would get even richer in the long run if they observed the niceties – right?

All the same, because the Cossack's project company was new and had no credit history, there were boxes that we had to tick. We'd received the letters from the regional governor, committing him to supporting the project. Narodneft had signed reassuring agreements about how much oil it would pump from its northern fields to the terminal once it was operational, and the export fees it would pay. We had statements of interest from prospective buyers for the oil in Holland and America. The banks had taken out political risk insurance (covering them in case of expropriations or coups). The main contract for the loan was watertight and oil-proof.

That wasn't quite enough for the banks to release the first tranche of cash. We also needed a report from Vyacheslav Alexandrovich the surveyor, confirming the suitability of the site chosen for the terminal and the progress of preliminary construction. We needed it immediately if the banks were to transfer the money – a hundred and fifty million dollars, I think, or thereabouts – before the end of the year.

The Cossack wanted the cash yesterday, he said he had liabilities to meet with his construction workers and suppliers. The bankers wanted to give it to him, especially because, if they waited until the following year, their bonuses for the closing one would be smaller. But there was a hitch. In the middle of December, Vyacheslav Alexandrovich had finally made it up to the Arctic. Then he disappeared.

In our office we worried that maybe he'd fallen through a hole in the ice or made friends with the wrong lady at the hotel bar. The Cossack said there were no holes in the ice and he was sure everything was normal. He wanted us to come to a meeting at Narodneft's Moscow headquarters, on New Year's Eve, to sign the last documents we had to send to New York and London before the banks released the money. Paolo agreed to go. He said he thought it would be a waste of our time, but we'd be on the clock even so. He took me and Sergei Borisovich with him.

* * *

Narodneft is more like a state than a company. Along with its wells and pipelines and tankers it has hotels and planes and football teams. It owns sanatoriums in the Caucasus and an island in the Caribbean. It runs a submarine in the Gulf of Finland and, rumour has it, a couple of satellites in space. It operates bespoke brothels and tame assassins. It was at that time said to bankroll half the members of the Russian parliament. It also boasts a weird HQ in southern Moscow that was built in the nineties, during what had evidently been the era of maximum eccentricity in Russian architecture, and looks like an inverted spaceship. Paolo, Sergei and I pulled up outside it first thing in the morning, at maybe half past eight. It was New Year's Eve, my last New Year's Eve in Russia.

Normally in the winter you can expect twenty or thirty seconds of leftover warmth, after you step out of a car or leave a building, before the heat of inside wears off and you suddenly feel the cold – a temporary delusion of comfort, like the extra time a decapitated chicken gets to run around before it realizes it's dead. You don't get that period of grace at minus twenty-seven. It was instant nostril-freeze and eye-water. (While I'd been away in England someone in the office had taken off a glove to answer his mobile in Paveletskaya Square, and the phone had frozen to his palm.) We hurried into the security cabin at the front of the Narodneft complex to have our passports checked, then up past the frozen fountains in the landscaped compound and into the main building. A ginger Narodneft 'greeter' in a green mini-dress showed us into the lift and wiggled us to a meeting room up near the spaceship's nose. The room had a sideboard set with vodka, glasses and bits of herring impaled on toothpicks, and a floor-to-ceiling view over the frigid city. The sky was as white as the snow on the ground, whiter maybe, because the exhaust fumes didn't reach that far.

The girl sat down on one of the chairs along the wall and smiled at us. Sergei Borisovich ate some herring. We waited, pretending not to look at her.

After maybe an hour, at about half nine, the Cossack came in. He was accompanied by two lawyers and a deputy director of Narodneft who seemed to be about nineteen. I found out later that he was the son-in-law of the head of Russian military intelligence. The Cossack whispered something to the girl and slapped her arse as she walked out.

'A little vodka?' he asked in Russian.

'Extreme,' said Sergei Borisovich, in English.

'No thanks,' I said.

'Come on,' said the Cossack, 'it's New Year's Eve.'

'First we work,' said Paolo, 'then we drink.' You could tell Paolo was a Moscow veteran if you knew where to look. He showed up at parties at midnight, at airports he charged to passport control like a stampeding animal to avoid the queues, he went outside to smoke when it was minus twenty degrees and he was never surprised.

'Okay,' said the Cossack. We sat down at the conference table. He whispered to one of the lawyers, who left the room for five minutes and then came back. We had a languid chat about legal technicalities. About twenty minutes later, Paolo's mobile phone rang.

'Maybe,' said the Cossack, 'this will be good news.'

Paolo answered it and walked over to the window to talk. I heard him say 'Where are you?' and some swearing in Italian.

He put his hand over the mouthpiece and asked what the phone number was in the meeting room. One of the Narodneft people told him, he repeated it and hung up.

'Vyacheslav Alexandrovich,' Paolo said, sitting down again. 'He's in Sochi.' You might already know this, but Sochi is on the Black Sea, about three thousand kilometres from where Vyacheslav Alexandrovich was supposed to be. 'He's calling back.'

A phone rang in the middle of the conference table. The Cossack reached over and switched on the loudspeaker.

Vyacheslav Alexandrovich told everyone he was sorry, please forgive him, it had been a family emergency, it would never happen again. But we shouldn't worry, he said: he had been up to the Arctic with his assistants, spent almost a week up there, in fact, and everything was normal. The construction team was ahead of schedule and on budget. They had started welding the pipeline that would run from the shore to the floating terminal, the first parts of the on-shore pumping station had arrived and were waiting to be assembled when the weather improved. The supertanker was in a dry dock along the coast and had begun to be converted (the hull adapted to take in oil from the pipeline on one side and pump it out to customers' ships from the other). They'd identified the locations on the sea floor where the twelve permanent anchors would be sunk.

All this was in his official report. He was wrapping it up now and it would be with us in hard copy very soon. He talked for about twenty minutes, spraying around measurements and statistics – decibars, barrels per day, metres per second, tonnes per year. He apologized again and rang off.

Paolo, Sergei Borisovich and I wheeled our chairs back from the table to confer.

'Is it kosher?' Paolo murmured to me.

'It's certainly convenient,' I said.

'And what is he doing in Sochi?' said Sergei Borisovich.

'On the other hand,' Paolo said, 'he knows what he is talking about. What is really the difference between a phone call and his report?'

'We have the other guarantees,' I said.

'And it's New Year's Eve,' said Sergei Borisovich.

I can't now remember exactly what we were thinking at that meeting. I'm sure we were eager to give the bankers what we knew they wanted, which was to make their problems go away and not discover new ones. We could see that the Cossack was a chancer. On the other hand, by the cowboy standards of that time it wasn't so irregular. We'd worked with Vyacheslav Alexandrovich before. All the paperwork was in order. Most importantly, Narodneft was behind the project, even if it wasn't legally responsible, and with its stock-exchange listing coming up we figured it had to care about its reputation. And for such a monster company the repayments amounted to small change: its executives probably dropped almost as much every year flying their wives to Paris for shopping trips in its private jets. Narodneft was behind it, and somewhere behind Narodneft was the President of Russia. We must have realized that Steve Walsh was right, and that the Cossack and his pals in the Kremlin or the FSB or wherever were bound to feather their nests a little. I'm sure we believed, though, that our banks would be safe.

In the end it was Paolo's call. 'Okay,' he said, 'let's do it.'

He went over to the window to wake up the lead banker in his Manhattan bed and tell him the good news. The Russians headed for the vodka and herring. We clinked.

Everyone was happy. The banks were happy, and so was Paolo. So was the Cossack. The Cossack was very happy. He invited me and Paolo to go hunting with him in the Altai Mountains. He said he would teach us to fire a grenade launcher. Which was my favourite James Bond film? he wanted to know. Was it all true about Freddie Mercury? Looking back I think he thought it was normal, his way of doing things – normal for us to drink together, make jokes and tell each other about our families, then do whatever had to be done anyway. I think he thought we were friends.

'So,' said the Cossack, 'Nicholas. When are you coming up to see us? Your new wife is waiting for you. Though on the other hand,' he said, 'I liked your Moscow wives very much too.' He gave me a quick, obscurely blackmailing wink, then knocked back another shot of vodka.

* * *

Paolo took us all for a celebratory lunch at Laughing Camel of the Desert, an Uzbek place on Neglinnaya. To get there Sergei Borisovich and I jumped into a passing Volga outside the tower at Paveletskaya. The enormous jovial driver was trying to learn English: he pulled an exercise book out of his glove compartment and pinned it to the steering wheel, every now and then writing down words that he liked the sound of ('lunch...Wild West...unsecured loan...leveraged buy-out...ExxonMobil'). He must have been driving by sonar. Outside the restaurant there was a shivering black doorman in a furry white costume. Inside, in the coat room, a pair of doomed cockerels scratched at their tiny cages, getting ready to peck each other's eyes out during the New Year's Eve feast. In the dining room there were two belly-dancers. One was a lithe thrusting blonde who looked more like an off-duty stripper than a proper belly-dancer, with a garland of hundred-rouble notes already sprouting from the top of her knickers. The other was a fat authentic brunette, wiggling each of her stomachs in turn, who no one was paying any attention.

Olga the Tatar was friendly, breathing on to my glasses and then polishing them, but I must already have been giving out spoken-for pheromones, either that or bad breath, because she gave up and concentrated on Paolo. Over the meal Sergei Borisovich told us about his efforts to dodge the draft, which in Russia seems mainly to be a pretext for mass sadism and slave labour. His family had two choices, he said: to pay the recruitment officer to let him off, or to pay a crooked doctor to declare him an invalid. They paid the officer ten thousand dollars, Sergei Borisovich told us, but the guy double-crossed them and drafted him anyway, so in the end they had to pay the doctor too.

'What did you think afterwards?' I said. 'About the army, I mean. And, you know, Russia. After the officer cheated you.'

Sergei Borisovich turned his potato eyes away and thought hard for about twenty seconds.

'Well,' he said, 'I probably should have paid the doctor to begin with.'

Then, just then I think, I saw her – I saw Katya. She was waiting the tables on the other side of the restaurant. She was wearing a short black waitress skirt, a plain white blouse and her hair in a neat plait. At first I wasn't sure that it was her, but then I was, and I got up and intercepted her as she was carrying the remains of a fruit platter back to the kitchen.

'Hello, Katya,' I said.

'Meet me outside in two minutes,' she said in Russian. 'The fire exit, next to the bar.'

It was suicidally cold in the street. Katya hugged herself against it when she came outside in her waitress outfit and someone else's coat.

'Kolya,' she said straight away, back in English and a little more poised, 'don't tell Masha that you see me here. Please, Kolya. Please. I need more money to pay for studies, but Masha is not knowing about job. She may be angry that I am not studying all my time.'

She put her hand, curled up inside her coat sleeve, just above my hip and looked at me without smiling. Another minute and we would have lost our extremities.

'Okay,' I said, feeling sorry for her, which must have been one of the things she wanted me to feel: sorry about this secret extra work, on top of her studies, sorry that she'd drawn a shorter straw than me in life. 'I promise. See you tonight.'

We went inside.

Later, as our taxi crawled back to the Paveletskaya tower through the traffic, I had one of those moments of semi-drunk reflection that at the time you can take for insights. They're just babies, I thought, these Russians with their blacked-out windows and their Uzis. All these adolescent hints of violence, from the bodyguards to the Cossack to the sabre-rattling President. For all their worldliness and pain, I thought then, the Russians are just babies.

* * *

'What a shame,' Tatiana Vladimirovna joked, as we all sat again in her overheated lounge. 'Such a winter, and no war.'

It was about nine o'clock in the evening on the same day, New Year's Eve. Outside, on the Bulvar and around the pond, teenagers were yelling and throwing firecrackers at each other. Katya had ditched her waitress outfit, and she and Masha were wearing skirts that told me we were going on somewhere afterwards. Masha had done her hair in a way I hadn't seen before, pulled back across her head with a ponytail at the back, with the tail wound around itself in a coil, which emphasized her green eyes and tight mouth. When we said hello she kissed me on the earlobe. Tatiana Vladimirovna had gone to town again with the buffet. When I gave her the stuff I'd bought for her in London – some Scottish shortbread, English chocolate and Earl Grey tea in a tin painted to look like a doubledecker bus – I thought for a second that she was going to cry.

She put the tea tin on the shelf next to the black and white photos of herself and Pyotr Arkadyevich. I'd sobered up from lunch at the Uzbek place just in time for the evening toasts. We toasted the New Year, and love, and Anglo-Russian friendship. When her blouse rode up as we lifted and clinked our glasses, I remember noticing that Katya had got her navel pierced.

We discussed the plan for the apartments.

Tatiana Vladimirovna was excited but nervous. Where would she buy her groceries? she asked. What if they never finished the Butovo place? It was true that she would like to get out of the city centre, she was too old, she was tired, but on the other hand she had been there so long, it was everything she knew.

Masha said that Stepan Mikhailovich was sure the building in Butovo would be finished by April. But to be extra safe, she said that they should wait until the end of May or the beginning of June to sign the final contract. Tatiana Vladimirovna would still be in there in time for the summer.

Next she explained that Tatiana Vladimirovna and Stepan Mikhailovich would have to obtain various important documents before they closed the deal. They needed proof of ownership for the two apartments and proof that the privatization of Tatiana Vladimirovna's place had been legitimate. They would need a certificate showing that her building was not due to be knocked down in one of the mayor of Moscow's architectural culls: the mayor would summarily condemn a building to death, and her brother would get a handsome commission to put up another one on the same site. They needed a document confirming that no one besides Tatiana Vladimirovna was registered to live in her flat – no one who was, say, away in jail, no estranged spouse who might turn up and claim his right of abode. (You still can't just live anywhere you like in Russia, you see, you can't just turn up like you and I did in Kennington. You have to register at a particular address, so the authorities know where to find you.) They also needed technical certificates for both apartments, which showed the floor plans, the plumbing, the structure of the buildings and so on. Finally they would need the legal contract itself. Normally, Masha said, all this was put together by a real-estate agent for a crazy fee.

'But, Kolya,' she said in Russian, 'you will help Tatiana Vladimirovna with the legal side, won't you?'

'Yes, of course,' I said. I'd promised I would in the *banya*, as neither of us had forgotten.

'You are a real English gentleman,' said Tatiana Vladimirovna. 'We are so lucky to have found you.'

'It's nothing,' I said.

We agreed that, on the day after the long New Year break, we'd go first thing in the morning to a notary, to get a power of attorney that would allow me to act on Tatiana Vladimirovna's behalf.

Just before midnight Tatiana Vladimirovna broke out a bottle of sickly sweet Crimean champagne. We watched the fireworks that were exploding above the magical building by the pond.

'May God hold you in the palm of his hand,' said Tatiana Vladimirovna.

We left as soon as we could without being rude, or maybe just before, and flagged down a car, driven by a spotty adolescent who was sixteen at the outside. He took us round the Bulvar and across Tverskaya, then up past the casinos on the Novy Arbat, shining out of the mid-winter night like an oasis in an Arctic desert, and across the frozen river to the Hotel Ukraina.

The hotel occupied one of the great gothic towers built in Moscow under Stalin, with grimy statues on the façade and, inside, Georgian gangsters, second-division Moldovan prostitutes and out-of-their-depth European school parties. We shuffled around to the side of the building on the icy pavement, the girls stabbing at the ice with their stilettos. At the back of the hotel we climbed up some fire-escape stairs and rang a buzzer. Masha repeated the password that she'd got from one of her colleagues, and we were let in to a giant speakeasy nightclub.

We emerged at about four – Masha back to my place, Katya

off on her own into the chilly New Year. I tried to get Masha to take me back to their apartment, but she wouldn't. She never did. At the time I thought that was just an ordinary version of shame.

| NINE

First thing in the morning on the first day after the New Year holiday – I guess it must have been 10 January or thereabouts – I went to the notary with Tatiana Vladimirovna, as we'd agreed, to get the power of attorney. Masha had to go to work in the shop that morning but Katya came with us. She was our chaperone.

Notaries are one of the staple Moscow professions, like property developers, Georgian restaurateurs and prostitutes. They are essentially pointless functionaries left over from tsarism, whose job it is to issue and stamp the legal documents that you need to do more or less anything in Russia. The ones the three of us visited that morning had an office hidden inside an old circus building, just to the north of the city centre. I guess that when the music stopped and the evil empire collapsed, and the Russians looked at each other for a split second before grabbing whatever they could, these notaries had somehow wound up with a room that had once housed a troupe of acrobats or lion-tamers.

We skated across the pavement outside the circus, Tatiana Vladimirovna moving quicker than I could over the ice, in her element in the winter like a penguin in water. We crept along the dark circus corridor and sat down in the notaries' waiting room. There was a big proud map of the Soviet Union on the wall. It was part of their job to make us wait, I think. Any Russian who has power over you (notary, ambulance man, waiter) is obliged to make you wait before they help you, so you know they can.

While we sat there Tatiana Vladimirovna told me how she'd come to the very same circus more than forty years ago. They'd had two elephants and a lion, she said.

'One of the elephants stood up on its back legs,' she remembered, smiling and holding up her hands like hamster paws to show what the elephant did, 'and when we saw that elephant we knew that we'd arrived in Moscow, Pyotr Arkadyevich and I. We knew Moscow truly was the capital of the world. An elephant!'

I asked her whether she'd missed Siberia or the village

outside Leningrad where she grew up.

Of course, she said. 'The forest. And the people. The people are different in Siberia. And in Moscow I also learned about other things, which maybe it would have been better not to know. It wasn't only elephants.'

Katya looked up from the epic text message she'd been composing and told Tatiana Vladimirovna not to bore me. I said I wasn't bored, it was interesting. That was one of the things I liked to think about myself in Moscow – that I was interested, concerned, nobler, somehow, than most of the other expat lawyers, who generally only stayed for two or three oblivious years, then retreated to service more reputable crooks in London or New York, sometimes as a partner in Shyster & Shyster or wherever, taking with them a handy offshore bank balance and some tits-and-Kalashnikov Wild East stories to console their live-long commutes.

I asked her how she'd lived through it all, Stalin and the war and the rest. It was a stupid question, I know, but the main one.

'There were three rules,' Tatiana Vladimirovna said. 'Obey these rules and it was possible to live, if you were lucky.' She counted them off on the stumpy wrinkled fingers of one of her hands. 'First, never believe anything they say. Second, don't be afraid. And third, never take any favours from anyone.'

'Except for the apartment,' I said.

'Except for the apartment.'

'What about the apartment?' said Katya, looking up again.

'Nothing,' Tatiana Vladimirovna said, smiling.

I asked her what she thought of the current weasel President (a mass murderer, like all Russian leaders as far as I can tell). She told me he was a good man, but he was only one good man against many bad ones, and he couldn't solve all the country's problems by himself. She hushed her voice and looked around, even though she was being polite. I said, didn't she mind that the people in charge seemed to spend half their time stealing? Yes, she said, of course she minded, but there was no point putting new people in the Kremlin, because they'd just start the stealing all over again. At least the ones in there now were already rich, so they could afford to think about other things too sometimes.

I asked her whether life was better now than before. She said yes, things were better, certainly for some people they were better. They were absolutely better for the young people, she said, looking at Katya and smiling.

We were quiet. Katya's phone beeped. She read her message, frowned for a moment and said, 'I've got to go.' She leaned in to me until I felt her breathing in my ear, and whispered in English: 'Please, Kolya, don't tell Masha that I go from you. I must to go to university.' Then she stood up and said, still in

English so Tatiana Vladimirovna couldn't understand, 'Kolya, remember, she is old lady and is sometimes making mistakes.'

She put on her coat and left.

There was only one other time when I was alone with Tatiana Vladimirovna, besides those fifteen minutes in the weird circus waiting room before the notary called us in. By the second time, I can see now, it was already too late, I was in too deep, had slipped too far from what I was before to what I was becoming. But I think, I hope, that on that January morning I hadn't yet, not quite. Things could – I'm sure, I hope – have been different, if I'd asked a couple of simple questions, instead of sitting there in silence, smiling and watching the slush from our boots slurp across the parquet.

In the end I asked her about Oleg Nikolaevich's friend.

'Tatiana Vladimirovna, I understand there is only a very little chance that you will, but I wanted to ask you, do you know an old man called Konstantin Andreyevich? He lives in the same area as me.'

'Just a second,' she said, closing her eyes and pressing her fingers to her temples. 'Konstantin Andreyevich ... I'm not sure. Who is he?'

'He is a friend of my neighbour Oleg Nikolaevich. We cannot find him.'

'No,' she said, 'I don't think so. I'm sorry.'

We were quiet again.

'Thank you again for the biscuits and the tea,' Tatiana Vladimirovna said to break the silence. 'It is excellent to have a speciality of England.'

'Maybe one day you will see England for yourself,' I said. 'Buckingham Palace. The Tower of London.'

'Maybe,' she said.

The notary called out, 'Next, come in.'

There were two women sitting behind a pair of desks in a narrow room. There was one window, I remember, looking out through rusty bars on to the white-grey street. It was a beautiful midwinter day, the sky as pure and glaring as the Mediterranean blue you and I saw on that holiday in Italy. The woman at the desk on the right was youngish, a sort of missing link between normal human beings and notaries. The older one, the boss – overweight, glasses, cardigan, hairy mole – was so rude that in another country you might have thought it was one of those hidden camera set-ups.

She took our passports and started to fill out the form for our power of attorney. She shrieked in glee when she saw that the name in my passport looked different to how I'd written it in her register, and seemed crestfallen when I explained that was because the passport showed my surname first. When she'd finished she stamped the two copies of the document she gave us about thirty times, pushed them across the desk without looking up and told us to pay her sidekick four hundred roubles. Tatiana Vladimirovna took one copy and I took the other. It meant that I could manage and sign all the paperwork for the apartment swap on her behalf. The apartment scheme was now my scheme too.

We slid back up to the Metro, so Tatiana Vladimirovna could go home and I could go to work, late. She said thank you and kissed me on both cheeks when we said goodbye. She waddled off towards the escalators.

For some reason it has stuck in my mind – in the way that things can without your wanting them to, sometimes, maybe especially, when you don't want them to – that down in the Metro, by the ticket kiosk, I saw two men having a row. One was a big Russian guy, the other a shaven-headed, furious, almost spherical Georgian, and the Russian was saying, over and over, very loudly, 'Give me the knife, Nika, give me the knife.'

* * *

That evening I found Oleg Nikolaevich waiting on his landing in distress. I could tell that he was waiting for me because he was coatless and hatless, not going out or coming in from anywhere. He was standing in front of his door, looking like a relative expecting bad news from a doctor. He tried to smile, and asked me how I was. I told him I was fine but very tired. He didn't budge.

'Nikolai Ivanovich,' he said, 'I must ask you once again for your help.'

I knew it was about the old man. 'Oleg Nikolaevich,' I said, 'forgive me, but what more can I do?'

'Please, Nikolai Ivanovich. Go to my friend's building. Just to look. I think there is someone in his apartment. I was on the stairs and I heard them coming down. Please.'

I looked into Oleg Nikolaevich's eyes, and he looked away. I could see he was embarrassed to ask me. In retrospect I think that for him the whole thing was less about his friend, in a way, than about resisting change, fighting time. I think he just wanted to keep his life as recognizable as he could for as long as he could – his friend, his cat, his books, his manners. I think that was why he stayed on in his downtown flat, instead of renting it out and living on the proceeds like most of the old Russians who had a pad like his (all their less tangible assets having vanished in the economic carnage of the nineties). Oleg Nikolaevich wanted to stop the clock.

'Okay,' I said in the end. 'Tell me where he lives.' He told me, and I can still remember: apartment thirty-two, number nine, Kalininskaya (a little turning between my building and the Bulvar that ran down the side of the church).

'So I turn right out of here, then take the first road on the left, and it's there, along from the church?'

'In Russia,' said Oleg Nikolaevich, 'there are no roads, only directions.'

* * *

I put my hat and gloves back on and went down the stairs. I walked up my street towards the Bulvar and turned into Kalininskaya. It was dark, and the only living things I saw outside were a gang of fat black crows convened around a rubbish bin. The ice that had formed underneath the drainpipes on the outsides of the buildings glistened blackly under the street lights.

When I reached the door of Konstantin Andreyevich's building I did what homeless people do in Moscow on fatal winter nights: I rang the buzzers of all the apartments, which the homeless try in the hope that someone will carelessly or compassionately or drunkenly let them in to sleep in the stairwells. Someone answered, told me to fuck off, but buzzed me in anyway, maybe by accident, and I climbed the stairs that curled around the caged elevator shaft to the third floor. I found Konstantin Andreyevich's front door.

I could hear him breathing. I rang the bell, and heard a man's voice mutter something and the squeak of his shoes on the inevitable parquet. I heard him stop maybe twenty centimetres from the door, and the creak of a leather coat as he leaned forward to look at me through the peephole. I could tell from his wheeze that he was a heavy smoker. He was close enough to shake my hand, or to slit my throat.

We stood like that, facing each other invisibly through the door, for what felt like a hundred years but was probably more like thirty seconds. Then he retched and spat. It was as though whoever it was felt obliged to go through the motions of pretending not to be there, but at the same time wanted to make it clear that he didn't much care if somebody like me knew that he was. I turned and headed down the stairs, slowly at first, then fast, two and three stairs at a time, the way you might run away from a bear, hoping it doesn't realize how scared you are.

On the ground floor I found an old woman collecting her post from one of the vandalized mail boxes.

'Excuse me,' I said in Russian, 'do you know who is living in apartment thirty-two – Konstantin Andreyevich's apartment?'

'The less you know,' she said without looking at me, 'the longer you live.'

'Please,' I said.

She turned to face me. She had sharp eyes and a white goatee.

'Who are you?'

'My name is Nicholas Platt. I am a friend of Konstantin Andreyevich.'

'Mee-ster Platt,' she said, 'I think it is his son in the apartment. That is what they told me.'

'Have you seen him?'

'Maybe.'

'What does he look like?'

'I can't remember.'

Outside, the wind was tearing through the canyons formed by the old merchants' houses, driving the snow into my face, making my nose run and my eyes weep. I forgot to put on my hat on my way back. If I'd dawdled I might have lost an ear. I scattered snow from my boots up the stairs of my building and rang Oleg Nikolaevich's buzzer.

'Oleg Nikolaevich,' I asked him when he came to the door, 'does Konstantin Andreyevich have a son?'

Oleg Nikolaevich shook his head.

Then, because we were still standing there, because I didn't know what else to say but wanted to say something, and because it suddenly occurred to me that I didn't know, I asked him what his cat was called.

'His name is George,' said Oleg Nikolaevich, turning away.

| TEN

'You know how they do it? How the serious guys do it? First they find some drunk or bum and give him five hundred dollars, a photo of the victim and the promise of another five hundred once he's done the job. The bum figures, what the hell, that's enough to keep me in meths or anti-freeze for a year. So he whacks the victim in his doorway or an alleyway with a knife or a hammer. If he's got ideas above his station, maybe he uses one of those air pistols they convert into real guns in workshops in Lithuania.'

'Why Lithuania?'

'Listen, that's not the end of it. This is the clever part, Nick. Afterwards the customer gives a pro ten thousand dollars to do the bum as well – tidily, you know, silencer, insurance shot to the head, deluxe. That way there's no living link between the customer and the original target. *Finito.*'

At that point, as I recall, Steve Walsh broke off to ogle two leggy redheads who were chasing each other round a striptease pole behind my left shoulder, one of them dressed as a rabbit (elasticated ears, furry white tail), the other as a bear (claws, bearskin bra, little brown bear nose). Russki Safari, I think the strip joint was called. It was Steve's favourite, somewhere out on Komsomolsky Prospekt.

'Wow,' he said, drinking up.

His riff on murder had started when I asked what had happened to the big energy story he'd been working on in the autumn. It was spiked, Steve said, after the editors got spooked by libel threats. But he'd been out to Siberia, to one of those obscure Russian districts that are three times the size of Europe. It was minus thirty-seven out there, apparently, and he'd almost lost his toes. He'd gone because the governor of the region had suffered a rush of blood to the head a month or so before: he'd launched a crackdown on corruption, annoyed someone in the interior ministry, and shortly afterwards had been found dead in the *banya* at the bottom of his garden. It was suicide, Steve explained, at least according to the prosecutor's office and the local newspapers. The governor had shot himself in the head – twice.

We both laughed. You learned to laugh, after a while.

So he had begun telling me how the Russian contract-killing market worked. The price had been going up, Steve said. You could try to hire a retired Chechen rebel, but you had to go through their friends in the Russian army who sold them the weapons, and that bumped up the bill. Otherwise, to find a competent murderer for less than ten thousand dollars these days, he reckoned, you had to go out to Yekaterinburg or down to Kaluga. Inflation, he said. Terrible, I said.

The bear caught the rabbit, or vice versa, and they set about eating each other. When they'd finished a blonde wearing only a pair of aviator goggles and high heels hung herself by her ankles from the top of the floor-to-ceiling pole. Steve took a happy swig of red wine.

I had, I suppose I should admit, been to flesh bars like that one too many times in my first year or so in Moscow – to Snow Queen, Pigalle, the Kama Sut-Bar. It was almost part of my job. Before, when I lived in London, I went to a lap-dancing place in Clerkenwell once or twice for stag nights, never otherwise, but in Moscow everyone with a dick and a credit card seemed to spend at least an evening a week shoving roubles into diamanté underwear, all the expat lawyers and bankers and half the Russian men who could afford it. By that winter, though, it had started to seem a bit demeaning – demeaning to me, I mean, not the girls. I don't think I really thought about the girls. Plus there'd been one nasty occasion when the barman loaded my bill with hyper-priced cocktails that I hadn't drunk, and when I argued the bouncers took me into a little yard outside the kitchen and swung me around by my hair for a few seconds, until my glasses fell off and I agreed to cough up. And by then there was Masha, and she'd been enough. I'd never felt that way about a girl for so long before. Usually, even when I liked them, my eyes wandered after a month or two. But Masha seemed to get better, fiercer, selfish in a good way. It felt like the real her and the real me, two mammals in the dark.

I hadn't spent an evening in that faintly gay strip-club atmosphere of shared half-drunk arousal for months. But Steve had wanted to go, so we went.

'How's the love of your life?' he asked me. 'The one you met on the Metro?'

'She's fine.'

'Has she moved in yet?'

'No. Nearly. I mean, not really. Not yet.'

'How about the babushka from Murmansk? When does she turn up?'

'Fuck off, Steve.'

It was, I think, the beginning of February. The snow was piled waist-high in the churchyard between my building and the Bulvar, even higher on the uncleared side of my street. Masha was fine, we were fine. She was probably staying with me two or three nights a week by then. I'd started laying in the food she liked, pickled mushrooms and berry juice and a Russian yogurty drink that I never got a taste for. I'd hired a Belarussian cleaner to keep the flat more or less hygienic. We were entering the stage when Masha might have moved in properly if we'd been in London, a city where, as you and I know well, practicality and the housing market nudge lust into commitment, mix up now and the future, and romance has a bottom line. Masha could go from Pushkinskaya Metro station to the mobile phone shop near the Tretyakov Gallery in a quarter of the time it would have taken her to get to work from the Leningradskoe Shosse. But she didn't mention it, and I didn't push her.

'She's got a sister,' I said to Steve. 'Katya. Blonde, nice girl. She's twenty. Sort of innocent and grown-up at the same time. She's a student at MGU. You'd like her.'

'Sounds like I would.'

'Except she isn't her sister, she's her cousin.'

'Right,' said Steve. Behind me the waitresses were massing on stage for their hourly 'jungle dance', wearing leopard-print mini-dresses and thigh-high snakeskin boots. I was losing him.

'It was strange,' I said. 'I went to that Uzbek place on Neglinnaya with some people from work. We went on New Year's Eve, after we signed some papers with the Cossack. Katya was waiting tables there. She didn't want me to tell Masha that I'd seen her.'

I hadn't told Steve about our first night together, the night Katya watched. I hadn't told anyone. I wanted to tell, like all men do sometimes. But more than that, I'd wanted to see Masha and us as something different, maybe even sort of pure.

'When you take them home and unwrap them,' Steve said inattentively, 'there's usually a piece missing.'

I started explaining about how I'd met their aunt, and about Butovo – how Tatiana Vladimirovna wanted to get out of the city, how I was helping. There were bureaucratic queues that had to be stood in, and agencies to visit that were only open for two hours every other Thursday. I had to turn up once or twice to sign for things, but as far as I could I'd delegated the leg-work to Olga the Tatar from my office – she'd bought her own little property not long before and seemed to know the form. I gave her the address of Tatiana Vladimirovna's place by the pond and of the new apartment in Butovo, since we'd need to check those papers too: it was apartment twenty-three, building forty-six, Kazanskaya. I promised Olga that I'd take her for cocktails in the rip-off bar at the top of the hotel next to the Bolshoi Theatre if she got it all together.

'It's not a lot of work,' I said to Steve. 'It won't cost me anything. And she's a nice old lady actually. She was in the siege of Leningrad.'

'Right,' Steve said. Tatiana Vladimirovna was at least fifty years too old to distract him from the jungle dance.

We watched. We were sitting in a grubby little booth to the left of the stage. After a few minutes the drumbeat stopped and the waitresses put their dresses back on. Steve clapped.

He asked about the Cossack.

'Do you know who he's fronting for? Your Cossack friend, I mean.'

'Who do you think?'

'Probably the deputy head of the presidential administration. Or the chairman of the security council. The St Petersburg crew are taking over, the old defence ministry gang are getting nervous. They're trying to cash out a bit while they can. I guess they'll keep a piece of the company they've set up to give them some pocket money later.'

'Maybe,' I said. 'We're not completely naïve, Steve. Maybe you're right. But the project's on track and that's all we care about. They're going to get the second tranche of money in the next few weeks and the last one in a couple of months or so. They think they'll be pumping their first oil through the terminal by the end of the summer. If they start repaying any later than next spring, the penalty clauses will kick in.'

'I'm sure you know what you're doing, Nick. But, by the way, I asked around. That logistics firm you said was in with Narodneft? It's a shell. No one's ever heard of it. I bet you the only sort of logistics it arranges involve pumping money to Liechtenstein. If you find out who the backers are, let me know.'

'Maybe, Steve.'

Three girls in Red Army fur hats marched around the tables, carrying replica machine guns (at least I think they were replicas) and wearing bullet bandoliers, draped carefully around their curves so that they covered nothing up. There was a lot of silicone and very little body hair.

'Aren't you heading down to the Caucasus?' I asked him. It was hotting up again down there, the TV news said, down in one of those fiddly little Muslim regions where there's always somebody rebelling and dying.

'Probably,' Steve said. 'Hard to sell the story though. The news desk in London's not too interested till there are three zeros on the death toll. And the Russians are trying to keep everybody out. You have to go down to Chechnya and pay your way across the border. Maybe next week. Shame to miss it.'

A couple of tourists disappeared into the cubicles next to the toilets, taking the rabbit and the bear with them. I'd done that too, or something like it, I suppose I should also admit, since I'm trying to tell you everything. Three times altogether, I think, I'd paid for it in Moscow. The first time was by accident, when I realized too late that I was expected to and was too far gone to stop myself, the other two times after I'd broken the taboo and thought, *Whatthehell*. Once, near the beginning, I'd managed to talk a catwalk Ukrainian into coming home for nothing even though she was working. Don't hate me for it. I would never do it in London. At least, don't hate me yet.

'Steve,' I said, 'do you ever think about this? I mean, worry about it – the way we live out here. I mean, what if your mother could see you?'

'My mother's dead.'

'You know what I mean.'

'Russia,' Steve said, looking me in the eye with his two bloodshot eyes and getting suddenly serious, 'is like Lariam. You know, that malaria medicine that can make you have wild dreams and jump out of the window. You shouldn't do it if you're the kind of person who gets anxious or guilty, Nick. You shouldn't do Russia. Because you'll crack.'

'I'm sure you told me Russia was like polonium.'

'Did I?'

He'd stopped listening again. His eyes were focused on the pole, around which a blonde in a Stetson and leather chaps and nothing else was lassooing a small herd of brunettes in cowhide bikinis. Steve waved at a waitress, tapping his empty glass for another hit of Moldovan Merlot.

ELEVEN

Tatiana Vladimirovna went out to Butovo again, with Katya I think, some time in the middle of February. I saw them all soon afterwards when we went skiing in the park at Kolomenskoe, down across the solid Moscow River. You didn't think I could ski, did you? You were right.

We left Tatiana Vladimirovna in a muddy little café by the entrance to the park, waving us away and ordering tea and blinis for herself. Masha and Katya brought their own skis, longer and thinner than the ones I remembered from my week of downhill when I was at university (drinking games, pissing in the chalet sink, a sprained ankle). I hired my skis from a kiosk beyond the gates, plus some felt boots that looked like they might first have been worn when the Russians invaded Finland.

By then the snow packed against the churchyard fence on my street had begun to resemble that multi-layered Italian dessert you like: whitish on top, creamy underneath, then a sort of stained yellow like leaked battery fluid, then a layer studded with rubbish (broken bottles and crisp packets and lonely discarded shoes, suspended in a gritty white lava), and beneath that, at the bottom, a base of sinister black slime. But at Kolomenskoe the snow was still white, stupidly white. It was hard and compacted beneath the top inch, and painful when you fell in it, which I did every time I went up or down an incline, once or twice losing my glasses and scrabbling around in the powder with my fat gloves to find them.

Masha and Katya seemed to be able to ski naturally, as naturally as they could walk on stilettos and dance. They laughed at me when I fell but went slowly till I caught up. In the park there was a wooden cabin in a grove of oak trees that was supposed to have been built by Peter the Great, and an old church, dedicated – as they always are – to some mythic victory over the Poles. The church was closed, and covered with scaffolding for renovations, but long pure icicles hung from the horizontal scaffold boards like necklaces of tusks. There was a man with a sledge, covered in bells and drawn by three white horses, offering people rides between the trees. The girls were wearing skiing kit, thin waterproof trousers and aerodynamic

jackets. I wasn't, and I got hot and wet at the same time. But when
we came out on to a ridge above a lake, frozen down below in
the middle of a leafless forest, it didn't matter. It was stunning.

When we arrived back at the café they went one at a time, I
remember, to change into their jeans and see to their hair in
the toilets while I thawed out with Tatiana Vladimirovna.

'Well done, Kolya,' she said when we were all sitting down.
'Soon you will be one of us. A proper Russian.'

'Maybe,' said Masha. 'He can't ski at all, but he loves the
banya.' She looked at me, smiling with one corner of her
mouth, a smirk of carnal triumph. I blushed.

Tatiana Vladimirovna told us about her trip to Butovo. It
didn't seem as if much work had been done on the apartment,
she said. But Stepan Mikhailovich had explained that they'd
been busy fixing the wiring, and the main thing, Tatiana
Vladimirovna said, was that it was nice there in the snow, so
nice, with the trails made by winter boots running between
the trees and around the pond in the forest opposite her new
building.

When she was a girl, Tatiana Vladimirovna went on, before
they moved to Leningrad, they'd made their own skis out of
bark. They'd laid down big bottles of pickles for the winter, cab-
bages and beetroot and tomatoes, and killed a pig in November
that they lived off almost till the thaw. Her family had been

poor, she told us, but they didn't know they were poor. I noticed a little blond moustache on her upper lip that I hadn't spotted before. I think she may have bleached it.

'You know,' she said, 'it is possible to see a church from the window of the apartment in Butovo. Do you know which church it is, Kolya?'

I'd seen the church she meant – the one with white walls and gold domes – but I didn't know which saint or tsar it commemorated.

'It is a very special church,' Tatiana Vladimirovna said. 'It was built as a memorial to the people killed by Stalin. They say that twenty thousand victims were shot near this church. Maybe more. Nobody knows exactly...I am not a religious person like my mother was, we lost all that in Leningrad. But I think it is good that I will be able to see this church from my window.'

I didn't know what to say. Masha and Katya were quiet too. The condensation on the inside of the café's windows was thick and streaked.

In the end Tatiana Vladimirovna asked, 'So, Kolya: will you have children?'

I'm not sure why – something to do with life going on, or needing to believe that it does – but the question seemed to follow naturally from the Stalin church and the mass graves. I tried not to look at Masha but I could sense her concentrating on her tea, turning away from me.

'I don't know, Tatiana Vladimirovna,' I said. 'I would like to.'

It wasn't really true. I'd always looked at acquaintances who'd become fathers with a mixture of contempt and animal terror. I'd looked at the babies, with their crawling and grabbing, their purposeful yet random tortoise movements, with no feelings at all. Don't worry, it's different now. I know you want children, it's settled.

That afternoon I just said what I thought Masha might want to hear, what most women want to hear. And if she'd told me then that she was pregnant, I might have wanted to keep it, I might even have been joyful – not because of the baby, but because it would have meant I was in with a shot at for ever. Though at the same time I wonder whether I knew, deep down, that we couldn't have a happy ending, whether in fact the nowness of it was what I liked about her most. I think I could see that there was something missing, or something extra, even if I was trying not to.

'I want children,' said Katya. 'Maybe six. Maybe seven. But only when I have finished my studies.' She was a simple soul, I thought, an open book, a fairy tale.

'And Masha,' said Tatiana Vladimirovna affectionately, 'I can see you as a mother.'

'I want children, yes,' Masha said in a low intense voice, without looking up. 'But not in Moscow.'

'Mashinka,' said Tatiana Vladimirovna, taking one of my hands in one of hers, and one of Masha's in her other one, 'if I could change one thing in my life, this would be it. Pyotr Arkadyevich and I, we were unlucky, and of course he had his work, and we had a good life together, but in the end...'

'That's enough,' said Masha, like she meant it, and took her hand away.

Tatiana Vladimirovna's eyes bustled between us from beneath her grey bowl fringe. Under our feet the floor was slippery with dying snow.

We ordered some vodka and 'herring in a fur coat' (marinated fish buried under a sludge of beetroot and mayonnaise). We talked about the arrangements for the apartment swap.

I said I was taking care of the property searches. I said I thought we'd have all the certificates we needed within a couple of weeks.

'Thank you, Nicholas,' said Tatiana Vladimirovna. 'Thank you very much.'

Then we talked about the money.

I think it was the first time they'd discussed the money in detail. Masha said that, because the new place in Butovo was worth less than Tatiana Vladimirovna's old one, Stepan

Mikhailovich was going to give her fifty thousand dollars. (People talked and thought and bribed in dollars in Moscow then, at least when serious money was involved, though when it came to it legitimate transactions were done in roubles.)

The truth is that fifty thousand wasn't enough. Flats in the centre like Tatiana Vladimirovna's were in demand from oil-drunk foreigners, as well as well-heeled Russians keen to set up their mistresses close to the office. There were bottles of wine in Moscow that cost almost as much as Stepan Mikhailovich was offering, and human beings who cost a lot less. But to Tatiana Vladimirovna fifty thousand dollars must have sounded as amazing as the twenty thousand people buried on top of each other under the snow in Butovo.

At first she said no, she wouldn't know what to do with so much money. Then she conceded that it was true, her pension wasn't enough, nobody's pension was enough – though on the other hand she had a little money saved from her job, and she got her special allowances from the state as a survivor of the siege of Leningrad, and a little bit more on account of her husband's contribution to the lost Soviet cause. All the same, she said, it might be nice to be able to go back to St Petersburg one day…

'Take it,' Masha said.

'Take it,' Katya said.

'Tatiana Vladimirovna,' I said, 'I think you should take the money.'

She scanned our faces again. 'I'll take it,' she said, clapping her hands. 'Maybe I will go to New York! Or London,' she said, and winked at me.

We laughed and drank.

'To us!' said Tatiana Vladimirovna, sinking her vodka in one. She smiled, and her fine skin, still taut over her high Russian cheekbones, looked for a moment like the skin of that happy girl in the photo from the Crimea in 1956.

*　*　*

That February – about a fortnight before my mother was due to visit – I caught a killer Moscow cold. It introduced each of its symptoms to me in turn, like musicians doing solos before they all join in for the finale: first the runny nose, then the sore throat, then the headache, then the works. Masha prescribed honey and cognac and no blow jobs. I had two or three days in bed, half-heartedly watching DVD box sets of American dramas, listening through the window to the street-scrapers and the prehistoric garbage trucks and, from downstairs, George's occasional sad meowing.

When I got back to the office at Paveletskaya, Olga the Tatar perched on the edge of my desk and ran me through the paperwork we had so far for Tatiana Vladimirovna's apartment. The privatization had been legal, one of the forms attested. Another one showed that the mayor had no current plans to tear down the building. A third demonstrated that nobody else had the right to live there. Tatiana Vladimirovna's husband was listed alongside her on one of the pieces of paper, but someone had crossed out his name and printed the word 'deceased' above it. We had the technical certificate with the dimensions of the rooms and the floor plan and the details of the sewerage and the power supply. All the forms were splattered with stamps, like blotches across a modern work of art. All this paper, I thought, and you still didn't own the place, not really. You never really own anything in Russia. The tsar or President or whoever is in charge can take it away, or take you away, any time he feels like it.

'What else do we need?' I asked Olga.

'Now you only need the transfer document from the property registration department. And the old lady needs to be examined by a doctor to prove she is not drunk or insane.'

This was necessary, Olga explained, because sometimes Russians sold their flats, but claimed a few months later that they'd been sozzled or high or deranged at the time of the transaction, and on that basis got the sale annulled and their apartment back. Or else some long-lost nephew turned up and claimed those things for them. In a Russian court you could prove anything for the right fee, but a certificate from a clinic would make it harder for anyone to try it on, she said.

I told Olga she was an angel.

'Not such an angel,' she said, but she sounded more sad than flirtatious.

'What about the Butovo flat?'

'For the other apartment,' she said, 'there is also some progress. The building has been constructed legally on the territory of the Moscow city government. In the old lady's unit, number twenty-three, no one else is registered to live. It is connected to the city drainage system and to the electricity network. The owner is a company called MosStroiInvest.'

I said I thought Stepan Mikhailovich owned the apartment.

'Maybe this MosStroiInvest is his company,' Olga said.

She held the forms above my head like bait. 'So, when do we go for cocktails?'

I thought of something Paolo had said to me soon after I arrived in Moscow. He said he had some bad news to tell me about being a lawyer in Russia, but also some good news. The bad news was that there were a zillion pointless, unintelligible and contradictory laws. The good news was that you weren't expected to obey them. I was sure there would be a way around MosStroiInvest.

'Soon,' I said, reaching up to take the papers.

Sergei Borisovich the potato face had come back from his winter holiday in Thailand, I remember, and he made us all watch a PowerPoint presentation of his photos. We were feeling virtuous, business-wise at least: we'd signed off the second instalment of the Cossack's loan and, according to Vyacheslav Alexandrovich the surveyor, at the current rate of engineering progress he'd soon be entitled to the rest of it. The Cossack had sent us a crate of live crabs (from the sea around the new terminal, he said). When I looked out of my window in the tower I could see a flock of snow-scrapers in orange overalls clearing the white rooftops on the other sides of the square, crawling along the inclines and reaching perilously into the gutters.

* * *

The central heating had baked my bedroom. I'd opened a window to let in some cold air and drawn the weird ruched curtains. Masha was on top, her fists scrunched into my chest, looking past my head and into the wall, breathing and concentrating like a middle-distance runner.

I hadn't seen her for more than a week. I'd been ill, and I thought she might have been away for a few days – her phone had been switching straight to voicemail – though she denied it when I asked her. I suddenly remembered what Olga had told me and worried and wanted to find out.

'What is MosStroiInvest, Masha?'

'What?'

'What is MosStroiInvest?'

'What?' She stopped her rocking and arching but she was still panting. 'I don't know,' she said.

'It's the company that owns the apartment in Butovo, Masha,' I said. 'The one for Tatiana Vladimirovna.'

She rolled off. She lay on her back next to me, looking up with me at the hieroglyphic lines on my ceiling. No part of us was touching any more.

'MosStroiInvest... I think it is company of Stepan Mikhailovich. Or of – how you say it? – the husband of one sister of Stepan Mikhailovich.'

'Brother-in-law.'

'Yes, company of his brother-in-law. Yes, I think this is name of company. Yes, MosStroiInvest.'

'It is better to be certain,' I said. 'Because otherwise there may be problems for Tatiana Vladimirovna.' There were lots of problems with Russian developers in those days. Sometimes they sold all the flats in a building, disappeared before it was finished, and the buyers built protest camps and set fire to themselves outside the government headquarters in the White House, up near the Hotel Ukraina.

Masha thought about it, her face turned away from me and

into the pillow. Her neck was flushed. My fingers had made red imprints on her ribcage.

'There will be no problems,' she said. She rolled on to her side so she was facing me, took one of my hands in both of hers, above and below, and looked into my eyes. Her eyes were jungle green. Her skin looked young but her flesh was tough, taut and muscled like a dancer's or a fighter's. 'And Kolya,' she said, more cold than tender, 'we ask you only to prepare papers for Tatiana Vladimirovna for selling her apartment. These other papers for Butovo, Stepan Mikhailovich will make. It is not needed for you to worry. We have all these papers already. For you it is necessary only to tell Tatiana Vladimirovna that all papers are in order. You must tell her this, Kolya.'

I said nothing. She touched me.

'Come back,' I said. That was all, but we both knew what it meant. I'd chosen to believe her. I'd taken her side.

'Okay,' she said, and she came back.

She is a special person, Masha. I have to tell you that. All that focus and self-control. I'm sure she could have been a great surgeon. Or maybe, in a different century, a champion nun. Or an actress – she would have made a great actress. She *was* a great actress.

* * *

People were skating on the deep-frozen pond the next time I went round the Bulvar to Chistie Prudy. There was a man leaving Tatiana Vladimirovna's flat as I arrived, a man I didn't recognize. He was fortyish, slick-looking, wearing a top-notch suede coat. Banker, I thought immediately. He had a signet ring on one of his little fingers and looked like he'd recently had an expensive haircut. He smelled of money. Katya was flirting with him as he tried to leave, smiling and twisting and sticking out her tits. The man said 'good evening' to me in Russian, turned up the collar of his coat and left. He didn't look to me like the sort of man who could have had a reason to visit Tatiana Vladimirovna.

'Who was that?' I asked as I took off my boots.

'I don't know,' said Katya, and laughed.

Straight away Masha slid across the parquet in her socks, grabbed us both by the hand and said, 'Guys, come to eat some blinis!'

The Russians were celebrating Maslenitsa, a half-pagan February festival, something to do with Lent, something allegedly to do with the end of winter, when the church bells ring and you eat pancakes. The three of us perched at the edges of Tatiana Vladimirovna's kitchen, eating blinis with sour cream and red caviar. The kitchen windows were sealed against their frames with masking tape to keep out the chill – an old

Siberian habit, I imagined, that she couldn't quite shake off. There were toasts.

'I have almost all the documents for this flat,' I told Tatiana Vladimirovna.

'Huge thanks,' she said, and kissed me on both cheeks.

'And Kolya is also preparing all the papers for your new apartment in Butovo,' Masha added, talking to her but looking at me.

'Excellent,' said Tatiana Vladimirovna.

I smiled and chose to say nothing.

| TWELVE

'I want you to meet my mother, Masha.'

'What?'

'My mother is coming to Russia next week. I am meeting her in St Petersburg on Thursday and bringing her back to Moscow on Saturday. She's staying here till Tuesday. I want you to meet her, Masha.'

'Why?'

I don't know why. I wanted you to meet her too, eventually, so you could see what you were signing up for (though I know you've never quite understood why her pettiness gets to me so much, which I guess is often the way with other people's parents). But that wasn't it with Masha. She never asked very much about my family, and I don't think I ever imagined a set-up in which both she and my parents featured prominently. Partly I think I wanted to show her off, to show my mum how complete my Russian life was without her and everyone else. Maybe partly I was trying to reassure her, offering Masha up as a witness to my contentment, and therefore to her moderate success as a parent. Or maybe I wanted and expected Masha to wear or say or drink the wrong thing, to do the work of anger and insult that I didn't have the stomach for myself. Perhaps I was even trying somehow to contaminate my mum with it, the stain that I darkly knew was coming. I think to Masha I was trying to say, look, no secrets, this is where I come from, come in, and at the same time, don't worry, this is not me any more, I've crossed over, look how far I've come.

'Only for an hour, Masha,' I said. 'Please. It will be nothing.'

'Okay, Kolya,' she said, 'I will meet your mother'.

'Thank you. I owe you one, Masha.'

'Okay.'

* * *

I doubt she really wanted to come. I think she must have experienced some late spasm of motherly anxiety, or at least of the feeling that she was supposed to be anxious. It may have been brought on by the thrum of bad news that was starting to beat out of Russia – the bombing on the Metro, the mysterious pipeline explosions and the thing with the ex-finance minister's helicopter. I wished some parallel, grown-up Nick and Rosemary could have talked about it honestly, said they loved each other in their way but agreed that it would be too much, five days, one hundred and twenty hours, with too little to say and at the same time much too much if we dared or bothered. But they didn't, and at the beginning of March, she came: my mother came to visit.

I waited for her at the airport in St Petersburg. It always looks, don't you think, like a lovely little moment of grace, the moment when you see a crew of happy strangers walking through arrivals, having flown through the air and landed alive – and at the same time somehow enviable and painful, the way they embrace their relatives, sometimes cry, then link arms and turn back to lives you know nothing about. Eventually my mother came through with the other British tourists. We kissed each other awkwardly, like politicians at a summit, and I found a taxi driver to take us into town. He was a retired army colonel, he told me, when I chatted with him on the way. He said he had a nice line in knock-off army clothing if I ever wanted some.

I'd booked us into a hotel at the wrong end of Nevsky Prospekt – one of those city-sized Soviet hotels with a thousand rooms, a bowling alley, a casino, an empty café on each floor and a brothel in the basement. The house prostitutes were chatting around the coffee tables in the foyer when we arrived. The front desk made me pay for both nights up front, a sensible precaution considering the state of the rooms (electricity cords looping across the ceilings like telegraph wires, and in the bathrooms no sinks and suspiciously damp brown carpet). My mum said she was tired, so we ate in the hotel. She made me ask whether the salmon on the menu was fresh: the waitress said it 'had only been frozen once'. There was a small posse of third-division mafiosi in the middle of the restaurant and a group of wobbly girls, who the men kept pushing out of their chairs to dance with each other between the tables, bullying the waiters to turn up the music.

When we went to bed someone kept calling me to ask whether I was bored, and would I like to be introduced to a very beautiful woman? I took the phone off the hook at about three in the morning, and slept until the late milky St Petersburg dawn – the northern light that makes you feel as if you're sleepwalking after you get up, or that you're already awake when really you're still dreaming.

We spent a day and a half looking at the Rembrandts and gilt in the Hermitage, scurrying along the frozen canals ('I didn't realize it would be *this* cold,' my mum said moronically), poking our noses into the yellow, malevolent St Petersburg courtyards, with their shivering cats and icy piles of rubbish. We nosed obediently around the churches, all besieged by beggars – drunks, crippled soldiers, drunks impersonating soldiers, real uncrippled teenage army conscripts who I imagined were working the streets to keep their officers in booze – and filled with icons, incense, woebegone headscarfed women and a haze of ancient prejudice. Plus the old addictive high, the crack for the soul that the Russian Church seems to push: the idea that life in this hard place could be beautiful.

I told her about my job, about Paolo and a little about the Cossack, but lost her when I tried to explain Narodneft and project finance. She told me she was worried about my father – not his health, she said, or not only his health. She started talking about their own childhoods, hers and my dad's. His father had come back from the navy after the war, she said, but had always been away somewhere in his head, and she thought now that might explain the distance between Dad and my siblings and me. She didn't go any further and I didn't press her. That's how it was between us that weekend: we kept starting conversations that might have led us into confidences or closeness, then steering away just in time. She went on and on about a very cold holiday she'd taken with her parents in Wales in the fifties, and how her father, who was a railwayman and who I never knew, made them all have a picnic in a hailstorm. It snowed as she talked. Her owlish glasses were constantly steaming up. She wore embarrassing boots.

Down by the river the Winter Palace glowed like a pink hallucination against the early sunset. The Bronze Horseman had dandruff. I stopped at a kiosk and bought Tatiana Vladimirovna one of those soppy snow globes, with a miniature St Isaac's Cathedral inside. In a funny way I think I missed her.

'It's a present,' I explained. 'It's for a woman I know.'

'I see,' said my mother. She looked at me sideways as we slipped along the pavement ice, beside a motionless canal. I could tell she wanted to insinuate something with her look, for it to be an adult moment between us. But she couldn't quite manage it, flustered, and looked away.

'No,' I said, 'it's for someone called Tatiana Vladimirovna, someone I know who used to live in St Petersburg.'

'Oh.'

'She's Masha's aunt.'

'Masha … is she the one who called you at Christmas?'

'Yes.'

'Ah. Good.'

We headed back to Nevsky Prospekt. It was about minus ten degrees. The winter somehow gets worse in March, I always found, because you can see the finish and you're desperate for it, like soldiers who become more scared when they know their war is about to end.

'It's nice that you're getting to know her family, Nicholas.' I think this was her way of asking whether it was serious.

'Just her sister so far,' I said. 'I mean her cousin. And her aunt. The aunt lives quite close to me in Moscow. She made us pancakes the other day.'

'Very nice,' she said. 'Lovely. Pancakes.'

I think maybe she was jealous of her – I think Rosemary was jealous of Tatiana Vladimirovna. I suppose she had reason to be. I'd spent more time with the old lady in the last few months than I had with my mum in the last four years. Which meant only one of them had seen what I'd become. Thank God I didn't introduce them.

* * *

We took the train home, the five-hour service that runs in the afternoon. Outside the station in St Petersburg there was an old woman standing in a raincoat, cradling a small numb-looking dog. 'Leningrad, Hero City' it says in big letters on the roof of the building opposite. On the train the two of us looked out silently at frozen bogs and trees, some standing and some recently felled in gritty cold clearings. Inside the carriage there was an aroma of Dagestani cognac, and the intermittent, varied ringing of mobile phones. A waitress came round with a trolley.

When I tried to order a beer and a glass of sparkling water she said, 'You can't be serious,' looking into my eyes until I asked for cognac instead. At the station in Moscow, half the human detritus of the lost empire seemed to have swept up around the statue of Lenin in the main hall.

We found a taxi to take us to my flat. 'Very cosy,' Mum said, peering around her from the entrance as if she was nervous to go any further, in case I had an opium den or an S & M dungeon set up in the living room. You know what she's like when she visits: struggling to seem relaxed, but judging and rearranging when you're not looking, quietly trying to make my place more like the family home. Making me feel like I'd never escape it. An hour later we went out to meet Masha at Café Lermontov – an overpriced restaurant done up like a boyar's palace, around the Bulvar from my road on the way to Pushkin Square.

Looking back I think Masha was ashamed that evening. I think she was capable of feeling ashamed. Somehow my mother was too much, not part of the arrangement. She wasn't rude exactly, just sort of shy and monosyllabic in a way that I hadn't seen before. She was wearing black jeans tucked into her boots, a black sweater and not a lot of make-up. She looked as if she was going on to rob a bank afterwards, or to change the sets in a theatre. Her outfit seemed to say, *I am not really here.*

'Nicholas tells me that you work in a shop,' my mother said over the tourist-trapski borsch.

'Yes,' Masha said. 'I work in shop selling mobile phones. Also calling plans.'

'That sounds interesting.'

Pause. Slurp. Distracting gaggle of top-of-the-range mistresses at a table in the corner.

'Kolya said me you are teacher,' Masha finally managed.

'Yes. I was a teacher in a primary school,' my mother said, 'but now I am retired. My husband was a teacher too.'

It was dumplings all round, and pirozhki (little Russian pies filled with meat and mushrooms), and not enough vodka.

'We're going to the Kremlin tomorrow,' I said.

'Yes,' said Masha. 'Kremlin and Red Square is very beautiful.'

'Yes,' my mother said, 'I am very excited.'

No dessert, thanks.

'Nicholas tells me that you are not from Moscow.'

'No,' said Masha. 'I am from city called Murmansk. It is most far from Moscow.'

'It's good that your family is here.'

'My family?'

'Tatiana Vladimirovna,' I said.

'Yes,' Masha said. 'Yes. We have aunt. Yes, it is very lucky.'

Masha looked away from us, out of the window and then up at the imitation eighteenth-century chandeliers.

'I hope one day we will see you in England,' my mother said, which I suppose she felt she ought to say, though maybe she was actually talking to me.

Masha smiled. The whole thing was agony, and then it was over.

* * *

The next day I took Mum to the Kremlin to see the tarted-up churches, the massive cracked bell that was never rung and the mighty cannon that was too big to fire. Two soldiers on the gates tried to tap us for a 'special' entry fee. Afterwards we went out to Izmailovo market, so she could choose some souvenirs among the chaos of icons, sperm-whale tusks, astronauts' helmets, Stalin paperweights, gas masks, samovars, Uzbek cotton, Nazi hand-grenades, Russian dolls depicting Britney Spears and Osama bin Laden, carpets, maltreated dancing bears and the sad fat freezing ladies singing 'Kalinka Malinka' for the tourists. She bought a furry hat for my father and a little jewellery box painted with a picture of a Russian forest for herself. I took the Monday off work and we went out to Novodevichy cemetery, where Khrushchev and other bigwigs are buried in gaudy tombs. Undaunted Russian children were hurling themselves on makeshift sledges down the slope from the walls of the adjacent convent, down to the frozen pond at the bottom, while the late winter sunshine bounced off the silver domes. We went to see Mayakovskaya Metro station on the way home, with its bright ceiling mosaics of zeppelins, parachutists and fighter planes, and the discreet hammer and sickle insignia sprinkled around them that no one has got around to removing yet.

In the evening we went to a classical music concert at the Conservatory on Bolshaya Nikitskaya, in the main performance hall, which has bad portraits of composers lined up around the walls. There was a bit of a scene at the beginning because two old women were sitting in our seats, and I could only get them to budge with the help of a ferocious usher. I don't remember what the music was. But I do remember glancing across at my mother after the interval, looking down into her lap, and seeing her hands joined together, and her thumbs twiddling round each other, and having a sudden sense of seeing her as if she was still a girl on a cold Welsh holiday – of seeing the person she was before she was my mother, and realizing how little I knew her.

We walked home, up Bolshaya Nikitskaya to the building that belongs to one of the lying Russian news agencies, with its big, aquarium windows, then along the Bulvar. Half the pavement in my street had been roped off with plastic tape, strung between metal rods like at a crime scene, to protect pedestrians from the lethal icicles dangling from the gutters with intent. The hillock of snow that contained the orange Zhiguli had the shape of a collapsed igloo or a burial mound, its surface dimpled with litter and spiky with half-submerged bottles and struggling twigs.

Oleg Nikolaevich was on his landing, carrying a bag that smelled of cat litter, smiling defeatedly like an aristocrat on a tumbrel. By then I usually tried to avoid him, truth be told, so I wouldn't have to talk about his missing friend, or see the disappointment in his eyes. I generally took the lift to avoid the spot he haunted, which I'm sure he noticed.

'Oleg Nikolaevich,' I said, 'this is my mother, Rosemary.'

'Very pleased to meet you,' said Oleg Nikolaevich in Russian. He took her hand and I think he was about to kiss it, but thought better of it. Then in his rudimentary English he said, 'How you like our Russia?'

'Very much,' she said, loudly as some English people do when they're talking to foreigners, as if they're all just a little deaf. 'It is a beautiful country.'

We stood there, suffocating in the uncontrollable central heating, goodwill and silence. Oleg Nikolaevich's eyes were badly bloodshot, I remember noticing, as if he'd been crying.

'No sign of Konstantin Andreyevich?'

'Nothing at all,' Oleg Nikolaevich said.

'How is George?'

'George is always unhappy in March.'

I said, 'And how are you, Oleg Nikolaevich?'

'In the kingdom of hope,' Oleg Nikolaevich said, 'it is never winter.'

I said goodnight, so did my mum, and we were turning away and upstairs when Oleg Nikolaevich dropped his bag of cat litter and grabbed the sleeve of her coat.

'Mrs Platt,' he said in English, in a funny sort of stage whisper, 'take care your son. Take care.'

* * *

Inside my flat my mum disappeared into the bathroom. Sitting in the kitchen I heard the taps running, the toilet flushing, teeth being brushed, the automatic unelaborate ablutions of a resigned sixty-something.

I'd given her my bed and opened out the futon in the spare room for myself. I heard her go into my room, then come out again and pad into the kitchen. She was wearing an old ankle-length nightie that might once have been purple or lilac but had been washed down to a gruel grey. She went to the fridge for some water, and stopped and turned back towards me on her way to bed.

'What did he mean, Nicholas? Your neighbour.'

'I don't know, Mum. He's upset because he's lost a friend.
I think he drinks.' I said this even though I didn't believe it.
As far as I know Oleg Nikolaevich was always sober when I
saw him.

She stood there in silence, but she was trying, really trying,
I could see that.

'Are you sure about that girl, Nicholas? About Masha.'

'Why?'

'It's just that she seemed...cold. Too cold for you maybe,
Nicky.'

'Yes,' I said, 'I'm sure.'

'Are you happy, Nicholas?'

It was the biggest question she'd asked me in about twenty
years. I thought about it. I answered truthfully.

'Yes,' I said. 'I'm happy.'

* * *

I owed Masha a favour, and she called it in.

It was, I guess, approaching the middle of March. There
was a crust like thick dried semen on the right wrist of my
puffy Michelin-man jacket, where for months I'd wiped my
nose as I struggled through the streets. I hadn't seen Masha for
a week or so, since the evening with my mother. I think she may

have been out of Moscow again, but, again, she didn't say so. I hadn't seen Katya for longer. The three of us met in a restaurant just off Tverskaya, on the other side from the stretch of heated pavement outside the mayor's office. It was still below zero, but Masha was already back in her autumn cat-fur coat. Katya was late.

'Did you like my mother?' I asked Masha.

'For me it was very interesting. She is – how you say in English? – scared. She is scared person. Maybe like you.'

She had her hair drawn back, tight across her scalp, and her eyes picked up the glow of the spotlights in the ceiling. She looked at me and I looked away. A waitress came and we ordered vodka and cutlets.

I said, 'How is your mother, Masha?'

'Not bad,' she said, 'but very tired. Coming old now.'

'I would like to meet her,' I said.

'One day, maybe.'

'How is your job?'

'I pretend work, they pretend pay me.'

Katya came in. She was only six months older than she'd been when I first met them, but it was a long six months for a girl of her age. She'd grown up into her hips and lips and pos-sibilities. They'd been a long six months for all of us – or long and short at the same time, as always with Russian winters, which always seem like they can never end and must go on for ever, right up until the warm moment when it feels as if they've never happened at all.

Katya took off her coat and sat down. Beneath her shirt I caught a glimpse of a new fuck-me tattoo on her hip bone.

'How is college?' I asked her.

'Good,' she said. 'Excellent. I am number two in class. Soon I will have exams.'

She gave us a long angry account of how, that evening, two men had got on to her tram and extracted ten roubles from each of the passengers by pretending to be ticket inspectors. Since almost none of the passengers had tickets, they all paid, even though they knew the men were fraudsters.

'Terrible,' said Masha.

'Terrible,' I said, as if this was the most terrible event any of us could think of, or wanted to.

They had two things to say to me that evening. One of them, the first one, the softener I realize now, was that around the end of May or beginning of June they were planning to go to Odessa for a long weekend, and would I like to go with them?

'You remember?' said Katya. 'From photos.'

The photos they'd shown me on our first night, at the floating Azeri restaurant at the beginning of the winter. Did I remember? 'Yes,' I said. 'I remember.'

They said they had a distant uncle who had a place out near the beach where we could stay. We'd swim and go to nightclubs. It would be 'class', Katya said. It would be perfect, Masha said. I said I'd love to go to Odessa with them.

The other thing they wanted to talk about was the money.

'Stepan Mikhailovich is having problems with money, money for Tatiana Vladimirovna,' Masha explained. 'Because of some questions with his business. He says it is very slow, this building. It is necessary to pay his men from Tajikistan. He can pay police to arrest all Tajiks – this is cheaper – but then he must find new workers. He can give twenty-five thousand for Tatiana Vladimirovna but for this other twenty-five there is problem. Of course Tatiana Vladimirovna does not ask for such money, and so Stepan Mikhailovich may simply say she will have only half, only twenty-five thousand. This way is easy. But we are thinking it is more kind if he is borrowing money to give to her.'

'Why doesn't Stepan Mikhailovich just give her the money later, when he's in the clear?'

'This also is possible,' Masha said. 'But, frankly speaking, after they change apartments I think Stepan Mikhailovich will think it is better he keep money than give it to this babushka. But if he is owing money to someone important then he may pay. Like if he will owe money to foreigner. Maybe to lawyer.'

It took me a while to work it out. Then I said, 'When? When will they need it?'

'They must make agreement for day of sale. I think it can be after two or three months. Maybe soon after Odessa.'

I'd never bought a house in London. I rented the place that I shared for a while with my old girlfriend (I pointed it out to you once, I think, on the way to a dinner party thrown by that woman from your old agency, I can't remember her name). I hesitated when house prices were on the way up, then decided to wait until they went south. I had quite a lot of money sitting lazily in my bank account, waiting for me to decide what to do with it, what I was going to do when I grew up. I earned a nice living, more than my parents ever could between them: not a lot by new Russian standards, maybe, but enough so I could spare twenty-five thousand dollars for a few months. I'd lent a bit of money to Russians once or twice before, in fact – a secretary at work, a Siberian girl I met at a party who wanted to buy a motorcycle – and always got it back. I thought I could pick them. With Masha and Katya I told myself that whatever was going on, we were on the same side. Though I think at the same time I was pleased to pay up, even relieved – because it made me useful, but more than that because I think I'd always known there had to be a price, and it had turned out to be only money, at least for me. As for them, I think they asked me for it just because they could, as if it was a sort of moral duty.

Masha said they needed twenty-five thousand dollars for Tatiana Vladimirovna. But it was also twenty-five thousand for that dinner with my mother, and in particular for the up-coming weekend on the beach in Odessa, maybe staying in the same room where Masha had taken the photo of herself in the mirror, almost naked, a picture that I can still see if I close my eyes, like an exiled believer can see a favourite icon.

'Okay,' I said. 'Tell Stepan Mikhailovich I am ready to lend him the money. Tell him I insist.'

'Okay,' said Masha.

'Okay,' said Katya, and poured.

'To us!' Masha said, and we clinked, her lips moistened by the vodka as it slipped into her, my throat burning and my skin clammy with apprehension, and the thrill my misgivings brought with them.

'I'm not scared,' I said.

* * *

When I got home that evening I found a smear of blood along the inside walls of my building, running up the stairs at about waist height. Outside one of the doors on the second floor the blood plummeted downwards, as if the person leaning against the wall and leaking it had collapsed there. Underneath there was a little bloody puddle, and next to the puddle a pair of old black shoes, standing neatly parallel to one another with their laces done up.

When I went downstairs in the morning the blood had been washed off the walls, but the shoes were still there. It was one of the alcoholics on the top floor, someone told me later. He fell. It was nothing to worry about, they told me.

| THIRTEEN

At the end of March the brown Moscow snow started to melt, then tried to freeze again when the temperature dipped for a day or two, living on as a nasty ooze – *sliakot*, the Russians call it – from which you almost expect a hairy prehistoric arm to reach out and drag you under. The pavement and kerb on the side of my street where the snow was piled up were slowly reappearing, the glacial heaps giving up their territory inch by inch. A single stained headlight emerged from the one in which the lost Zhiguli was buried, winking out like a muddy blood-shot eye.

It was the end of March, or maybe the very beginning of April. We met at Tatiana Vladimirovna's place so she could sign the preliminary contract papers that I'd prepared, using the power of attorney she'd given me: her place by the pond to be exchanged for the new one in Butovo, plus fifty thousand dollars, on a day in early June. I walked around the Bulvar to her apartment through the afternoon slush. In the underpass at Pushkin Square, I remember, there was an old man playing the accordion with a spaced-out kitten on his lap, but I was hurrying and I didn't give him anything.

I was early. Maybe I was early on purpose, wanting to get there before Katya and Masha without really knowing why. It was only my second time alone with Tatiana Vladimirovna, after those few minutes in the waiting room at the notary, when Katya had got a better offer and left us. It was that afternoon, before the girls showed up, when I found out that she was not and never had been their aunt – not an aunt in English, not in Russian, not an aunt in any language. It was my last chance.

I took off my shoes. She'd already started to pack. Cardboard boxes were stacked along the parquet of the corridor, unsealed and stuffed with papers and trinkets (the arm of a candelabra stuck out of one of them, like a cadaver's arm from a coffin), plus one or two of those enormous patterned bags that you see immigrants lugging around airports. But in the lounge nothing seemed to have been touched yet. The photos of her lithe Stalinist self and her dead husband, the musty encyclopaedias and the medieval telephone still sat there like exhibits in a 'how they used to live' museum, along with my bus-shaped box of English tea. The phantasmagoric animals watched me from across the pond through the soup of an afternoon. Tatiana Vladimirovna brought tea and jam.

I gave her the corny cathedral snow globe I'd bought for her in St Petersburg. She smiled like a baby, then kissed me and put it on the desk in between the telephone and the photograph of her husband.

She asked me whether I liked St Petersburg. The truth was that I'd found it stressful and vaguely spooky, but I white-lied and said I did, it was very beautiful, the most beautiful city in the world. I can't now remember whether I prompted her, or whether she just started on her own, the conversation receding naturally from my visit to her past, but that day we talked about the siege.

She said that when she thought about Leningrad now, it was always cold and always snowing – she looked over at my gift and smiled – though she knew that some of the time she was there it must have been summer and hot and light. Of course, she said, St Isaac's wasn't a cathedral then. The communists had turned it into a museum of atheism, or a swimming pool, she couldn't remember which, she must be losing her mind.

'Everything,' she said, 'was turned upside down. At first we listened to the radio and it told us we were heroes, and that Leningrad was a hero city, and we felt like heroes. But then people became animals, do you understand? And all other animals were food. We had a dog, he was only a little dog, and we hid him from the other people. But he died anyway, and in the end we ate him ourselves. It would have been better to eat him when he was fat!'

She laughed, a short, fierce Russian laugh.

'The richest people were the people who had the most books,' she said. 'They burned them, do you understand?'

'Yes,' I said, though of course I didn't.

'Books were for burning. Dogs were for eating. Horses were for eating, sometimes when they were still alive. They fell down in the street and people ran with knives. Boots and shoes were for making soup.'

She paused, sort of swallowed, always trying to smile.

'I was in a basement…I remember after the war, in the children's camp, they gave me an ice cream. They told me I was lucky.'

I said, 'Would you really like to go back to St Petersburg?'

'Maybe.' She closed her eyes for about five seconds, then opened them. 'No.'

I asked whether Masha and Katya's family had been in Leningrad with her during the siege.

'I don't know,' she said. 'There were many people in Leningrad. More at the beginning, of course.'

'Didn't you live together?'

'What?'

'I thought you might have lived together?'

'Why would we have lived together?'

'Because you were family.'

'Family? No, they are not my family.'

Yes, I was surprised, though maybe not altogether surprised. But in that moment I chose to hide it. I chose to turn my last chance down.

'I'm sorry, Tatiana Vladimirovna,' I said. 'I made a mistake. I thought you were their aunt.'

'Their aunt? No,' Tatiana Vladimirovna said, shaking her head but smiling, 'I don't have any family now. Nobody.' She looked away from me and rocked slightly in her seat.

'How do you know them, then?' I asked her as calmly as I could. I didn't want to alarm her but I wanted to know the facts. 'How do you know Katya and Masha?'

'It was very strange,' she said, shifting her buttocks on the sofa like she was settling in for a long and gripping story. 'I met them on the Metro.'

* * *

I'll come back to Tatiana Vladimirovna, I promise, but I want to flash forward again, just by a few hours. I want to tell you what happened later that day. I think it will help you to understand the way I was behaving. Assuming you want to understand. It helps *me*: looking back, the two meetings feel part of the same event, one little revelation spread over an afternoon and evening.

After we left Tatiana Vladimirovna's, I went with Paolo to meet Vyacheslav Alexandrovich the surveyor and the Cossack. It was a Sunday, I think, but we needed to see them urgently. The banks were due to release the last and biggest tranche of the loan the next day: two hundred and fifty million dollars, give or take the odd million. The Cossack invited us to an office building on the embankment, near the old British embassy and across the river from the flesh-coloured walls of the Kremlin. It wasn't his office, we found out later. I doubt the Cossack even had an office then. He just had a Hummer, his chutzpah and his *krisha*.

We went up in a mirror-walled lift to the third or fourth floor, to a room with an imposing conference table and windows overlooking the river. It was late afternoon and gloomy, but you could see how down below the ice on the river was buckling and cracking, great plates of it rubbing and jostling each other as the water shrugged it off, a vast snake sloughing off its skin. Down along the embankment the yellow and grey buildings disappeared into the dirty sky, the lights of the upper windows flashing out of the murk like low-flying UFOs.

There was vodka (plus some black bread and pickles, for the sake of appearances).

'Something to drink?' said the Cossack, heading for the sideboard.

'Just one,' Paolo said.

'Okay,' I said.

'No thanks,' said Vyacheslav Alexandrovich.

Paolo knew him from the previous time he'd worked with us, but I'd only met him once before, at the beginning of the winter, when we signed him up for the oil terminal job. He was a short, pale man, with thick hair, thick Soviet glasses and worried eyes. I suppose if you wanted to you could say he looked like a sort of compressed or stunted version of me. His suit smelled of cigarettes and Brezhnev. I remember he had scrunched-up bits of cotton wool plugged into his ears, a precaution some superstitious Russians take if they go outside when they have a cold.

The vodka bottle was shaped like a Kalashnikov. The Cossack picked it up by the butt and poured four large shots. When he held my glass out towards me I saw that his cufflinks were miniature dollar bills.

'Something to drink,' he said to Vyacheslav Alexandrovich, telling him not asking, as he gave him the glass he hadn't wanted.

'To us!' said the Cossack, knocking his back in one, then wiping his mouth on the back of his funeral-black sleeve. Paolo and I clinked and drank. It was top quality, smooth, no after-burn, almost no taste.

Vyacheslav Alexandrovich took a sip and smiled thinly.

'Drink it,' said the Cossack, not smiling.

Vyacheslav Alexandrovich took a deep breath, like a diver going under, and downed it. Afterwards he gasped, his mole eyes blinking and watering behind his glasses.

The Cossack laughed and slapped him on the back. They must have been about the same height, but the Cossack had a heavy prison-weightlifter build, and Vyacheslav Alexandrovich was all slouch and paunch, with one of those ill-fitting bodies that are somehow fat and skinny at the same time. He shot forward, then steadied himself and tried to smile again.

'Well done,' said the Cossack. 'So, let's sit down.'

We were there to certify the papers the banks needed before they could write the final cheque or push the money-transfer button. We each had laminated copies of the letters of assurance from the Arctic regional governor. We had those promises of high-volume oil deliveries from Narodneft. The banks had their political risk insurance and our comforting book-length contract. But we needed Vyacheslav Alexandrovich's latest progress report.

I took notes. Everyone else smoked, Vyacheslav Alexandrovich inhaling in a hurry but looking less relaxed with each drag. He told us that the supertanker had been fully converted, and the tugs were about to tow it out to the loading site. The twelve anchors that would hold it in place had been sunk, the sea floor had been prepared. He stood up and talked us through a presentation that he projected on to a screen on the wall. It included scale drawings and photos of relentless bits of spiky equipment burrowing into mud. There was one of a stretch of pipe lying half buried in the ice, like a negligently disposed-of corpse, and a blurry image that was supposed to show the bottom of the Arctic Ocean. The presentation stalled at one point, and I could see the sweat standing out on Vyacheslav Alexandrovich's neck and nose as he pummelled the computer to get it to start up again.

In conclusion he said he was confident the equipment was in place for reliable oil exports to commence very soon. At the end he looked down at the table and smoked like his life depended on it.

The Cossack said, 'Good news!'

Paolo and I conferred. I was distracted that evening, it's

true. But it was mostly a formality anyway. It was too late for us to advise the banks to back off, even if we'd wanted to. And we didn't want to: Vyacheslav Alexandrovich seemed thorough and Narodneft was still onside. We didn't confer for long. Paolo said he thought the banks should release the funds. I agreed. We told the Cossack.

'Okay,' he said, twitching his fringe.

But the main reason I remember that evening – the reason it has melded with my chat with Tatiana Vladimirovna earlier, the reason I want to tell you about it – is not the meeting itself or the expertly casual torture I watched the Cossack inflict on Vyacheslav Alexandrovich. It's what we did afterwards. It was the only time I ever saw Paolo really angry, even including what happened later, and the only time we ever argued, he being a man whose purpose in life had been to transform arguments into agreements, find acceptable forms of words, gloss over unpleasant realities.

We wrapped up our business. The illuminated Kremlin palaces were glaring at us from across the river and through the sudden night. The Cossack invited us to dinner to celebrate. 'And after dinner,' he said, 'who knows?' His eyes flickered with rape, pillage and money-laundering schemes.

Vyacheslav Alexandrovich made his excuses and left. Paolo, the Cossack and I walked down the street to the Cossack's tinted-window Hummer. Paolo turned up the collar of his Italian coat. I remember the Cossack was wearing one of those fur hats, made from some endangered animal, that sit on top of Russian men's heads and leave their ears exposed, just to show how butch they are. Inside the car he had a plasma television, a fridge and a driver with a purple scar down one cheek. The driver lowered the window, letting in the sharp late winter air, and with his other hand reached underneath the front passenger seat and produced a blue police light which he slapped on to the roof. He pushed a button and we set off through the dusk and along the river with our blue light flashing – past a hotel with a two-hundred-dollar Sunday brunch and up to the House on the Embankment, the bad-karma building where Stalin's henchmen lived in the thirties, until they didn't, and which by then had a giant rotating Mercedes sign on top. At Kropotkinskaya, along the outer wall of the cathedral, a line of old women was standing and moaning hymns under the yellow street lights, waiting to see whichever repatriated icon – some lock of saintly hair or scrap of holy kneecap – was on display inside. They looked unreal, like extras on a film set, there in that city of neon lust and frenetic sin. We got stuck at the lights, and the Cossack swore and kicked the back of the driver's seat.

On Ostozhenka we pulled up outside an elitny restaurant-stroke-club. Absinthe, I think it was called. The blue light was switched off. There was a line of would-be oligarchesses shivering in the pavement slush, hoping to be smiled on by the resident *feis kontrol* supremo. The crowd parted for the Cossack as the traffic had made way for his flashing light. He was carrying one of the leather man-bags, just big enough to hold a small semi-automatic, that were then all the rage among the muscled and moneyed classes in Moscow – accessories so camp they were somehow threatening, like they were daring someone to try to steal them. He pulled something out of the bag, waved it at the bouncers and entered the promised land. We strode in behind him and gave our coats to the pretty cloakroom attendant.

'What was that?' I asked after we sat down.

'What?' said the Cossack, summoning a waiter with a commandingly lazy finger gesture. The air was thick with smoke, Russian techno and the aroma of deluxe women.

'What did you show the bouncers?'

He opened his bag and took out a card with a double-headed eagle on one side, and on the other a photo ID. It stated that he worked for the economic affairs secretariat in the Kremlin. He twirled his contraband card between his fingers. 'Forbidden,' he said, 'only means expensive.'

We ordered cocktails, and when they came the Cossack stood up to make a toast, then another and another: 'To our friendship...to our cooperation...may your families prosper...may our countries always be at peace...may you come to visit us in the north.' A Russian toast is a liquid dream of a different life.

'There is something I wanted to ask you,' I said.

'Anything,' said the Cossack, spreading his arms wide and making innocent eyes.

'Have you heard of a company called MosStroiInvest?' I was curious.

'MosStroiInvest? MosStroiInvest...No, I think no. Maybe, yes maybe. Why?'

'I have a friend who is buying something from them. An apartment, I want to know if they are reliable.'

'I understand,' the Cossack said. 'I will make enquiries, okay? I will ask my friends in the construction business and let you know. Next week probably. Okay?'

'Thank you.'

'Now,' said the Cossack, 'there is something I want to ask you, my friend. About those girls.' He wagged a finger at me.

'Which girls?' said Paolo.

'Have you had one,' the Cossack said, 'or both? Maybe both together?'

'They are sisters,' I said.

'That makes it more interesting,' said the Cossack. I think

they were trained to do this, the Russian spooks: to find out something about you, to pick up some little snatch of nothing, then to use it against you, so you wondered how they knew, what else they might know, who they might tell, and you worried.

'Are they good girls, Nicholas?'

'I think so, yes.'

'Be careful,' said the Cossack. 'Sometimes, in our Russia, people can be less kind than they seem. You get me?'

The Cossack's phone rang (his ringtone was 'The Final Countdown'). He answered it, mumbled something, then made one last toast, the Moscow flatheads' favourite: 'May the dick be hard, and may there be money!' He gave his credit card to the waiter, kissed us both on both cheeks, said 'ciao' to Paolo and left.

I never saw or spoke to him again, not counting a couple of times, months afterwards, on the TV news – during the latest war in the Caucasus, after he'd become deputy defence minister – when I thought I glimpsed him smirking in the background as the President addressed the wrathful Russian nation.

'Barbarian,' I said under my breath, or maybe it was something less polite.

Whether it was because he thought I was wrong, or because he secretly felt I was right, or because his wife was bullying him for a new-model BMW or a facelift, or for some other reason that I couldn't fathom, Paolo flipped.

'You think you're so different to him, Nicholas?' He bared his teeth and looked suddenly old in the mauve restaurant light. His grammar seemed to buckle. 'Mr English Gentleman, you think they do things so much differently in London? Yes, they are more subtle, *ecco*, more nice, more clean' – here he mimed washing his bony hands – 'but it is the same. In Italy also. In everywhere the same. Strong and weak, power and no power, money money money. It isn't because of Russia. This is life. My life, Nicholas, and your life also.'

Maybe I was thinking about what I hadn't said to Tatiana Vladimirovna earlier. Part of me may have needed to pretend – still, that night more than ever – that I was better than I was. Better than I am. I told him I thought he was wrong. I said we weren't the same. We had rules, we had limits. I said I wasn't the same.

'No?' said Paolo. 'So I tell you one more thing, Mr English Gentleman. This Cossack is how we make our bonus, understand? No Cossack, no bonus. You are sure you are different? You are sure? You and me, we are the fleas on the Cossack's arse.'

There was more. Paolo had a drop of brown blood in the yellowy white of his eye. After a while I couldn't argue any more. I looked away and out of the window towards the cathedral's ridiculous dome. Teenagers were smoking and kissing in the slush around the statue of some forgotten revolutionary.

That was the lesson, the same lesson, really, as I learned at Tatiana Vladimirovna's: that we were no different. I was no different. Perhaps I was worse.

I raised my almost empty cocktail glass and said, 'To putting lipstick on a pig!'

'Okay,' said Paolo. 'To the pig's lipstick!'

We clinked.

* * *

They met on the Metro, Tatiana Vladimirovna had told me, just as Masha and I had. She said she'd been at Dorogomilovskaya market buying carp – which, I remember her mentioning, she would bring back alive and keep in her bath – and the girls had helped her with her bags at Kievskaya station. I imagined them flanking her in the hall between the platforms, beneath the misleading mosaics that portray Russian-Ukrainian friendship. It happened in June, Tatiana Vladimirovna said, and I could picture the two of them in summer frocks and open smiles, charming and strong, and Tatiana Vladimirovna sweating in a short-sleeved summer blouse and a too-heavy skirt.

She said that they had truly come to feel like family, even in this little time. But no, she said, she wasn't actually their aunt. I sat there kneading my hands and said nothing. My hands looked like somebody else's hands. I guess they figured an aunt would sound more plausible, less incriminating, and that if they were careful they could keep it from coming out.

'Don't worry,' Tatiana Vladimirovna said, smiling, 'it's not important.' Looking back, I wonder whether maybe she was trying to say, *Don't worry about any of it.*

I was drifting towards forty. I'd drifted to Moscow and to Masha and into this. It was only another drift, to pass over this lie and live with it. It wasn't even such a difficult one, to tell you the truth. Probably the truth – the truth about me, I mean, and how far I could go – was there all along, very close, waiting for me to find it.

I changed the subject. I drank my tea. I said I was very glad the winter was nearly over. I said that we were thinking of going to Odessa. When the girls arrived neither of us said a word about what Tatiana Vladimirovna had told me. She evidently chose to forget about it too. She gave us cake and chocolate. She signed the forms she needed to sign.

Later I withdrew twenty-five thousand dollars from the bank, and Masha and I met Stepan Mikhailovich at an empty jazz club near the Conservatory, with dark private rooms, to hand over the money (he theatrically declined to count it). I told Olga the Tatar not to worry about collecting the papers for the Butovo apartment. We had those, I told her. I took her to the fancy bar in the hotel next to the Bolshoi like I'd promised.

FOURTEEN

In my experience you could roughly gauge the level of depravity in a Slavic city by the time it took, after you arrived, for someone to offer you women. In Odessa, I didn't make it out of the airport. As we were walking to his car from the Soviet arrivals terminal the taxi driver asked me whether I wanted to meet some girls. The fact that I already had two girls with me didn't seem to deter him.

It was, I think, the first weekend in June. Just before we flew out of Moscow it snowed again – the end-of-May, fuck-you snow by which God lets the Russians know that he hasn't finished with them yet. But, inside, the Flintstones plane baked like a *banya*. Somewhere very close to my ear a high-pitched engine whine got steadily louder and made it seem inevitable that, in the end, we must crash. I sat across the aisle from a mad, fat, Hungarian businessman, who for the first half hour of the flight stared at me and cursed in four or five languages like he was looking for a fight. Then he calmed down, wiped his forehead, and complained about the changes in Ukraine since the new President took over (maybe you saw him on the news – the guy with the ruined face, from when the Russians tried to poison him). Ukraine, according to the Hungarian, just wasn't corrupt enough any more. 'Six months ago,' he said plangently, 'I knew who, when, how much everything took. Now it is impossible to get anything done.'

The plane smelled of sweat and cognac. A stewardess stationed herself outside the toilet at the back, ready to turn off the smoke alarm for a small consideration. Two drunk Russians danced a jig in the aisle as we came in to land, while the passengers around them clapped.

The early summer Black Sea warmth licked at my skin as we stumbled down the steps and across the cracked tarmac. It wasn't properly hot, not yet, but it felt like paradise. I got an old childish sensation of out-of-placeness, a feeling I remembered from our two or three family trips to the Costa Brava – a glow of forgiven naughtiness at having made it to a place that wasn't really mine, at having somehow got away with something.

I had. I was in Odessa: technically in Ukraine, but for Russians still a fairy-tale nirvana of debauchery and escape. Masha and Katya were strolling in front of me in mini-dresses and strappy high-heeled sandals that they'd put on while we were in the air. They were wheeling knock-off Louis Vuitton cabin luggage, wearing film-star sunglasses, willing smiles and, I was almost sure, no knickers. Masha put up a bright red sun umbrella that wiggled in synchrony with her arse.

They looked like they were celebrating. They had almost done it. Or we had almost done it. By the time we went to Odessa there were just a couple of visits to a bank before it was all over.

The Ukrainian border guard had trouble deciphering my exotic passport. An old woman standing behind me in the queue tapped me on the shoulder and asked long-sufferingly, 'Do you have to pay him, young man?' In the end the guard brandished his stamps and I went through customs to catch up with the girls. I found them in the arrivals hall, negotiating with the taxi driver (gold incisors, year-round leather jacket, shiny shoes that looked pointy enough to pick locks with).

We were heading for the car park when he asked me.

'Do you want to meet some girls?'

I laughed like a nervous foreigner. Katya laughed too.

'Do you?' said Masha, in a voice I didn't recognize, ironic

but also somehow angry and mocking and final. 'Do you want to meet some girls, Kolya?'

* * *

They'd turned off the central heating in Moscow about five weeks before we went to Odessa, some time towards the end of April. I was at home with Masha – she was wearing my dressing gown and watching reality TV, I was enjoying some light foreplay with my new BlackBerry – when we heard the tell-tale snap in the heating pipes, short but distinct: the starting gun for the summer, for the urgent squeezing of life and lust into a few little warm months. The big melt was on, the snow and ice running off the roofs like low-altitude rain. Foreigners smiled at each other in restaurants, like speechlessly relieved survivors of a catastrophe. It was over: the back-and-forth between over-cooked buildings and frigid streets, the endless putting on and taking off of clothes, the marathon Russian winter that no sane human being would voluntarily live through. It felt like a miracle.

We were having a warm, mellow period too, Masha and me. It wasn't real, I can see that now, maybe I could even see it at the time. But in a way it was the most real time, the most honest. It was still love, though by then you could also have called it an addiction. I do need to tell you these things, I think.

I'm sorry if they hurt.

We talked. She told me about the winters of her childhood, and the gangster warfare that had gripped her city in the early nineties, the mayor's hoods on one side, she said, the governor's thugs on the other. When one of the gangsters got killed, she recalled, his friends would put up a life-size statue of him holding his car keys in the cemetery: people called them 'memorials to the victims of early capitalism'. She told me about how as a teenager she'd longed to get to Moscow, or if not Moscow then St Petersburg, and failing that maybe Volgograd or Samara or Nizhny Novgorod, somewhere civilized, she said, anywhere where they'd have jobs and proper nightclubs, somewhere else. I told her things too, stuff I've never talked to anyone else about, except maybe you. Not secrets, exactly, I didn't have many of those then. More, you know, feelings and fears – about my job, my future, how I'd wound up alone.

We even talked again, but more like it was a script or a game, about her coming one day to live with me in England. Though it had started to seem doubtful that I would ever manage it myself: I'd begun to feel like one of those hopeless colonials you hear about who stay too long in Africa and can't survive when they wind up back in Blighty. I no longer had a picture in my mind of what life in London would be like, with no snow, dachas and drunk Armenian taxi drivers. I'd lost my idea of me. I had long-term expat syndrome, which is maybe, I think, just an extreme version of the unmooring that seems to dizzy some people in early middle age. Masha was adrift too, in her way, but she seemed to know where she was going.

Two or three times I went down to meet her after her shift in the shop, and we went for a stroll on the embankment or a drink in the Irish pub on Pyatnitskaya. Once we went to look at the icons in the Tretyakov Gallery, sliding around in those silly plastic slippers that they always make you wear in Russian museums, me feeling embarrassed until I registered that everyone else was wearing them too. Masha knew the names of all the saints, and which unlucky city it was that Ivan the Terrible or whoever was sacking in the pictures, but she wasn't really interested, and I was only pretending. She seemed tender, sometimes at least, spooning with me afterwards and once or twice putting on one of my badly ironed shirts to bring me coffee in the morning.

Thanks to Olga we had almost all the papers for Tatiana Vladimirovna's old flat. Just before Victory Day, Masha, Tatiana Vladimirovna and I went to a psychiatric clinic to get the last one – an official declaration that she was of sound mind when she agreed to the deal (Katya was studying for her exams, Masha said, and didn't come). A babushka, a hard beautiful gazelle and a bespectacled foreigner: a suspicious combination, I imagine, to anyone who might have noticed us.

* * *

Every underground system has its official and unofficial rules. In London, on the Tube, you must stand to the right on the escalators, let disembarking passengers off the trains first, never talk to strangers and never kiss in the carriages before breakfast. In Moscow, after the stop before the one you're getting off at, you must rise and stand motionless facing the doors, formed up with the other exiting passengers like soldiers waiting to go into battle, or Christians into a Roman arena. Then you force your way out on to the platform as the take-no-prisoners grannies elbow their way in.

The day we went to get the certificate we stood up at Krasnoselskaya and got off at Sokolniki. Outside, a few ridges of ice sheltered in the gutters, moulded against the crumbling kerbs, and a few little black-grey lumps clung to the bases of street lamps. The pavement looked like it had been doused in chilled gravy. But the girls were back in their short skirts. The streets smelled of beer and revolution.

The clinic we'd chosen crouched in a maze of shabby seven-storey Soviet apartment blocks. Fat unburied heating pipes snaked around and between the buildings, like the outside of that arts centre in Paris, but less colourful and padded with asbestos. We went in, past the smoking nurses in the lobby and up two flights of stairs to the psychology department. There was a faint smell of gas and a distinct sound of dripping. We saw two patients in hospital gowns, one of them also wearing a broad straw hat. The psychologist had a framed certificate on his wall, John Lennon glasses and three-day stubble. On his desk he had a pile of loose papers, an old red telephone and two plastic cups, one of them lying on its side. There was blood on his white coat.

'Does she drink?'

'No,' I said.

'No,' Masha said.

'Doctor,' said Tatiana Vladimirovna, 'I am not dead yet. I can answer your questions myself.'

'If she drinks,' the doctor said, 'it is still possible to obtain the certificate. Only it will be a little more expensive.' He folded his hands on his desk and smiled.

'I am sober,' said Tatiana Vladimirovna.

The psychologist wrinkled his nose. He wrote something down. He looked disappointed.

'Drugs?' he said hopefully.

Tatiana Vladimirovna laughed.

'Who are you?' he said to me, suddenly prickly with propriety.

'I'm her lawyer,' I said.

'Lawyer? I see.'

The psychologist shuffled his papers. He moved on to the sanity test.

'What is your name?' he asked Tatiana Vladimirovna, leaning forward across his desk.

'Iosif Vissarionovich Stalin,' said Tatiana Vladimirovna. She held her poker face – or maybe it was her interrogation face from the old days – long enough for the psychologist to perk up, thinking he might have a pretext to up his fee. Then she said, 'That was a joke.'

She gave her real name, her date of birth, the name of the weasel President, and one or two other answers that most genuine lunatics could well have come up with. We paid four hundred roubles, plus another three hundred for (according to the psychologist) the secretarial work. We took Tatiana Vladimirovna's certificate of sound mind and left.

After that, I only saw her once more before we went to Odessa. This time I am sure of the date. It was 9 May: Victory Day.

* * *

I invited them over to my place – Masha, Katya and Tatiana Vladimirovna. We would watch the parade of tanks and missiles in Red Square on television, then stroll up the Bulvar to Pushkin Square to watch the commemorative fireworks shooting over the Kremlin.

It was a lovely afternoon. Masha and I laid on blinis, smoked salmon and the rest. That day she let me feel that we were like other couples, couples who have you round to dinner and show you how happy and speechlessly effective they can be together, how competently in love, how bickeringly at ease. After the parade, the radio played patriotic songs, and Tatiana Vladimirovna taught us some wartime dances, a waltz I think it was, and another one I can't remember. First she danced with me, while Masha clapped and Katya laughed, next she showed each of the girls in turn. Then we moved the Ikea coffee table in my lounge to the side of the room and we all danced together, mostly me paired with Masha in her light green summer dress, and Tatiana Vladimirovna with Katya. Tatiana Vladimirovna was sweating and smiling and flinging Katya around like she was a teenager, and once or twice she let out a high, strange peasant shriek, a noise that seemed to come from somewhere in the back of her throat and deep in her memory or her genes.

Finally she bent over, panting, as the three of us flopped on to the sofa. 'Bravo, kids,' she said. 'Bravo. And thank you.'

I'd always thought it was a bit sick-making, the obsession the Russians have with the war. But that afternoon I could see that Tatiana Vladimirovna's friskiness was nothing to do with Stalin and the eastern front or anything like that. It was about lost loves and youth, and defiance, and going to Yalta in 1956.

After the dancing, Masha brought out the documents.

'Tatiana Vladimirovna,' she said, 'I wanted to let you know. Kolya has gathered all the papers for your new home in Butovo. The statement of ownership, the technical certificate – everything necessary to prove the sale will be legal and without any problems. Here.' She held up and spread out a sheaf of papers like a St Petersburg duchess with a fan. 'And we also have all the documents for your flat, which Stepan Mikhailovich will need to see.' She held up the file Olga the Tatar had put together and that I'd given to her earlier.

'Show them to her, Kolya,' Katya said, smiling.

'Yes, please, Nikolai,' said Tatiana Vladimirovna. 'I am sure they are all in order but I would like you to explain them. Then I will be absolutely comfortable.'

'Here you are, Kolya,' said Masha, and she held out her fan of papers and the file.

The document that you cannot buy in Russia has yet to be invented. At Paveletskaya, in the underpass that leads from the Metro to the silly tower where I worked, you can buy college diplomas, residence permits and certificates that declare you are a qualified brain surgeon. Sometimes the fakes are actually real, in the sense that they are drafted by corrupt officials of real universities or in the mayor's office or the Kremlin administration (there is a lively market in blank paper left over from the nineties, on which backdated contracts can be made up with period watermarks). Some of them are glaring counterfeits. I don't know where Masha got the documents for Butovo that I saw for the first time that afternoon. They were convincing enough, with all the right insignias and a rash of plausible stamps. There was something funny about the signatures maybe, and the shadow that a photocopier sometimes leaves in one or two off-white corners, but nothing too obvious or alarming.

I laid out the paperwork on my kitchen table and sat down at it with Tatiana Vladimirovna. We ran through the documents for her old flat first. Then I showed her the one that listed the amenities of the building in Butovo, and the one showing how nobody else was registered to live in the flat that was supposed to be hers. And the one that identified Stepan Mikhailovich as its current rightful owner.

It was a nice afternoon, and it would have been a shame to spoil it. We were going to Odessa and it would have been a shame to spoil that too. It would have been tricky to go back from where we'd already got to. But the reality was worse and simpler than any of those explanations. It felt like almost nothing, I have to tell you, when I took Tatiana Vladimirovna through those documents on Victory Day. It felt inevitable, almost natural. I know how it must sound, but there's nothing else I can say.

'Excellent,' she said when we'd flipped through them. 'Nikolai, you are like an angel.'

'Yes,' said Masha, 'Kolya is our angel.' She ran her hand through my hair, very lightly, just once.

'You're welcome,' I said.

'Let's go,' said Katya, standing up and stretching. 'It will soon be time for the fireworks.'

* * *

We ran into Oleg Nikolaevich on our way out that night. We took the lift down past his floor, but he was coming in through the building's front door as I went to open it. He was wearing his black suit and a white dress shirt, like he was a jazz musician or an undertaker, and carrying a briefcase which, I was fairly sure, was empty. Masha and Katya were behind me, Tatiana Vladimirovna behind them.

I congratulated him on his country's great victory, as the Russians do on Victory Day. He congratulated me on Great Britain's victory too. 'Glory to your grandfather!' he said. I'd told him once, when we used to talk more, about the convoys and my family's Russian connection.

'Oleg Nikolaevich,' I said, 'let me introduce my friends,

Masha and Katya.'

'Yes, yes,' he said, as if he recognized them. 'Your friends.'

'Happy Victory Day!' Katya said, and giggled. They were like cagey members of different civilizations, who just happened to speak the same language.

'Yes,' said Oleg Nikolaevich. 'And to you too, girls.'

'So,' said Masha. 'It's time for us to go. Excuse us, please.'

Oleg Nikolaevich flattened his body against the wall to let the girls pass. They brushed past him and went out into the street. 'All good things,' he said quietly.

Tatiana Vladimirovna was still inside and standing next to me. I couldn't think of how to explain who she was, so I just said her name.

'Pleased to meet you,' Oleg Nikolaevich said.

'Me too,' said Tatiana Vladimirovna.

I saw the wariness in both pairs of eyes, felt them sizing each other up for background, education, the quantity of blood that might have been washed off their hands or their families' – the sort of instant epic calculations that older Russians make, a bit like the way English people weigh up each other's shoes and accents and haircuts. Then their eyes softened, their shoulders relaxed, the guards dropped.

'And I congratulate you too, Tatiana Vladimirovna,' said Oleg Nikolaevich.

'Sixty years,' said Tatiana Vladimirovna. 'Is it sixty?'

'More or less,' he said.

I suppose she must have been six or seven years older than him, but they'd both lived through it all – the war, Stalin, the whole Russian nightmare. They were both old enough to have believed in something, even if the thing they'd believed in had turned out to be a sham. The younger ones, most of them, had nothing to believe in even if they had wanted to. No communism, no God. Even the memory of God had been forgotten.

'We went to Kazan,' Oleg Nikolaevich suddenly said. 'On the Volga. My father was a technician in a physics laboratory. We were away from Moscow for two years.'

'Leningrad,' Tatiana Vladimirovna said, just the name of the city, nothing else.

Oleg Nikolaevich nodded.

We were moving away and out of the door when he said, 'One minute, Nikolai Ivanovich. One minute alone, please.'

Tatiana Vladimirovna went out into the almost warm dusk to join the girls while he and I stood in the doorway. The women were a few metres away from us. I guess they could have heard what we were saying if they had strained and if they had wanted to.

Oleg Nikolaevich said, 'They are putting in a jacuzzi.'

'Where?'

'In Konstantin Andreyevich's apartment. Someone has moved in.'

I hadn't thought about Oleg Nikolaevich's friend for a long time, and if I'm honest I didn't much care to.

'Who?'

'I don't know. I don't know. A woman I know who lives in the building told me. She saw it.'

'What?'

'The jacuzzi.'

He waited for a reply, but I had nothing to say about the jacuzzi or his friend. I think probably he just needed to tell someone. I'm sure he knew it was too late to expect much help from me any more. Just as it was too late for his opinion to make a difference to me and the girls.

To end the silence, I told him that I was going to Odessa for a few days at the beginning of June.

Oleg Nikolaevich looked into my eyes, then out for a moment towards Masha and Katya in their strappy dresses. When he spoke he seemed to be addressing a point somewhere along my collar bone.

'Invite a pig to dinner,' he said, 'and he'll put his feet on the table.'

* * *

We watched the fireworks from Pushkin Square, Tatiana Vladimirovna standing between me and Masha, our arms interlocked with hers. She liked being around lovers, I think, even if not much of the love was for her. Katya had a packet of sparklers that she handed out and we waved them at each other. When the bangs started we looked up into the sky above the Kremlin and said 'oooh' and 'hurrah'.

'Enjoy yourselves, kids,' Tatiana Vladimirovna said when she wished us goodnight, and blew us all kisses, and winked at me.

* * *

I took another day off work and we flew to Odessa on a Friday morning. In the end the place on the beach fell through, if it had ever existed, and we stayed in a hotel. I paid, naturally, and in return I got to act out the whole big-shot routine, checking in with the two of them, turning up for breakfast with them. The hotel was on a lovely lazy avenue, crowded with blossoming trees and statues of dead Odessans, above the grand old steps down to the seafront. It had a fine wooden staircase, a restaurant that must once have felt like the Ritz and a beautiful view of the early summer sun swimming in the oil-dark sea. It brings it all back, telling you about it like this.

We took a room and a half – a big bedroom with a single-bed children's annexe and a shared bathroom. Katya went out straight away to stroll and flirt. I admit it, I asked Masha to drop her dress, open the wardrobe door and stand in front of the mirror, like she did in the photo they showed me at the very beginning. Only now I was sitting behind her, looking at her back in front of me and her front in the mirror and myself in there with her. Our eyes met somewhere in the door, the images of us close in the glass but our real selves separating, already far apart.

I sat and she stood like that, only our eyes speaking, until Masha said to the me in the mirror, in the same violent voice that had come out of her at the airport, 'Is it enough, Kolya?' In Odessa she was attentive, punctual, courteous to the needs she'd got to know. But it was as if she wasn't really there, or maybe as if I was already not there, inside her head, and per- haps because I wasn't there she could afford to be generous with me.

We got dressed. At the top of the steps down from the shady avenue to the sea we found a dwarf crocodile, a balding owl and a nervous monkey, waiting to have their photos taken with suggestible tourists. It was warm in the sun but almost cold in the shadows. The Odessa cafés were opening up for the sea- son, unfurling their umbrellas and letting down their awnings like animals stretching themselves after hibernation. Bashful

American men chatted awkwardly about the menus with the online brides they'd flown in to meet. There were two girls circulating in knee-high PVC boots and suspenders, giving out leaflets for a strip club. I'd been wrong, maybe, to have thought their religion was dying, these flamboyantly sinful Slavs. Maybe to be this immoral you've got to have religion somewhere – some decrepit gods lurking at the back of your mind, gods you are determined to defy.

In the middle of the afternoon we took a taxi out to the beach.

I asked Katya, 'How were the exams?'

'What exams?'

'Your exams at Moscow State University.'

'Yes,' she said. 'Exams. They were excellent.'

We were sitting at a little bamboo beachside café. Lean teenage boys were hurtling into the cold sea water from rickety waterslides and the end of a broken-down pier. From a distance the sand looked like the kind I once saw on a volcanic beach in Tenerife (a long time ago, before you, before Russia). On closer inspection it appeared to be mostly cigarette ash. Katya was wearing a transparent dress with a red bikini underneath. Masha was twirling her sun umbrella. I couldn't see her eyes behind her sunglasses.

'What subjects did you take, Katya?'

'Business...economy...and many more.' She smiled. 'I am very good student.'

'First in class,' said Masha, and they laughed. I laughed too.

The concrete path that ran behind the beach smelled of piss, but somehow not too objectionably. An old man was tending a punchball game, and a mournful old woman offered to weigh us on a set of old-fashioned scales. There was a pile of snoozing dogs. There seemed to be almost nothing to hide now. They weren't sisters. Tatiana Vladimirovna wasn't their aunt. Katya worked as a waitress in the Uzbek restaurant. Everything was coming out.

We sat on the beach (Masha and Katya spread out plastic bags beneath them to protect their clothes). We agreed that in the evening we'd go back to one of the beachfront nightclubs that we'd walked past. We bought three ice creams from a woman who seemed to me to look like Tatiana Vladimirovna, and licked at them in silence.

I found out about Seriozha at the hotel, when we were getting ready to go out again.

* * *

Masha retreated to the bathroom and locked the door. The taps ran. Katya fell asleep. I could see her lying on her front through the door of her room, with her arms straight by her sides like a corpse. After about a quarter of an hour I knocked and asked Masha whether she was all right, and after a long pause she said '*da*', drawing the word out in a voice somewhere between an orgasm and a death rattle. I turned on the television: I found a weightlifting contest, soft-core adverts for Italian chatlines, a scrum of men in tight suits attempting to throttle each other in what I think was the Ukrainian parliament, and a strange military ceremony, involving a brass band and some camels, transmitted live from Turkmenistan. I switched it off. From somewhere behind the hotel I heard what I amateurishly took to be two gunshots. Then I saw Masha's pink-trimmed purse sitting on the side table by the bed, picked it up and looked inside.

She had both passports, the international one plus the internal kind that Russians have to carry around with them. That's how I can be sure of her surname. Afterwards I realized that I could have found and written down her address. Perhaps I should have, but I was in a hurry and careless and I didn't. She had a membership card for a gym and another for a nightclub in the Taganka district that I'd never heard of. She had a discount card for an accessory shop on the Novy Arbat, three stamps on a 'buy six get one free' card from a coffee shop at Pushkin Square, a Metro pass, about two thousand roubles and fifty dollars. I found a scrap of paper with her phone number on it, which all practical Muscovites carry, so that anyone who stole the purse could get their granny to sell Masha's identity documents back to her a couple of days later. She had a photograph.

He looked too innocent, the little boy in the photo. It was black and white, passport size, but I could make out a Tintin blond quiff, the hair curling out of a winter bonnet that was tied under his chin. I couldn't tell for sure – the monthly stages and cute accomplishments that parents get so worked up about have always been beyond me – but I reckoned he was about a year old in the photo. You could only see his top half, but he seemed to be wearing a miniature sailor suit. He was half facing the camera, half glancing up at the woman whose lap he was sitting on. It was Masha.

I turned the photo over. Someone had written 'With Seriozha' on the back, and a date. It was about five or six months before I'd met her. I calculated that at the time of Odessa he must have been about two years old, that little boy. I put the photo back in the purse and the purse back where I found it.

* * *

They both wore cat-suits that night – Masha's dark blue, and Katya's, I think, purple – and too much make-up. We went for dinner at a Ukrainian buffet. I piled my plate with dumplings, but ate almost nothing, just sat there thinking, *Who is Seriozha?* *Who is Seriozha? Who is Seriozha?* They talked about where they'd go on holiday if they could afford it (the Maldives, the Seychelles, Harrods). Afterwards we had a pina colada in a heaving bar, then took a taxi out to a nightclub on the beach. Rameses, I think it was called, or Pharaoh.

It was the first weekend of the season, early in the evening, maybe ten thirty, and cool. The place was half empty. There was a stage drowning in dry ice, a bereft dance floor and around it tables climbing the sides of three plastic Egyptian pyramids. We sat down and waited for something to happen, not bothering to try to talk above the techno. Slowly, then all of a sudden as parties and nightclubs tend to, the place filled up. Masha and Katya went off to dance. I headed for the bar and stood there on my own, looking and drinking.

Apart from a dozen or so central-casting gangsters with fear-me black jackets, tree-trunk necks and death-row haircuts, I was the oldest person there by roughly fifteen years. The leggy Odessan women looked at me in my jeans and party shirt like I was a flasher or a beggar. There was a strip show – a weird nude ballet featuring an immobile male hulk and two disappointingly long-in-the tooth, saggy-in-the-tits women. The ironic clubbers cheered and whooped.

When the strippers picked up their clothes and scuttled off

I climbed a pyramid and scanned the dance floor for the girls. It isn't altogether clear for me now, that night, but in my dreamy memory of it I fought my way over to their spot in the corner by the stage, apologizing inaudibly to the owners of the toes I trod on, my glasses sweating, my ears pounding. They'd teamed up with another girl and a boy, I remember, but the strangers retreated into the jungle of limbs when they saw me coming.

I stood in front of Masha, grabbed both sides of her head to keep it still, and shouted as loud as I could.

'Who is Seriozha?'

'What?' Her face stopped dancing but her body tried to carry on.

'Who is Seriozha, Masha?'

'Not now, Kolya.'

'Is Seriozha your son, Masha?'

'Not tonight, Kolya.'

'Is he with your mother? Was your mother really ill when you were young? Do you have a mother, Masha?'

'Not tonight. Tonight is for you, Kolya. Let's dance, Kolya.'

Her body started up again. I still had her head, but she reached around me with one hand for Katya, and then I felt Katya's arms pushing over my shoulders and her fingers mating with mine at the back of Masha's skull, and Katya's breath on my neck and her firm front pressing into the middle of my back.

I was half-full of pina colada, and the other half of me was drunk on understanding. I let Katya pull away my hands, stopped shouting at Masha and swayed into my usual school-disco shuffle. We must have looked like a cheesy male fantasy.

But the thing about Odessa, even more than in Moscow, is that in the right light, with the right lubrication, you can somehow make things seem better than they truly are. You can make things be what you want them to be. People live on that, and so can you. So did I, for that long last night. The dry ice cleared, and I saw the shimmer of the Black Sea beyond the nightclub stage, and the crests of the waves on their way in to find us by the moonlight. It seemed to me that I could dance, dance like the bodies twisting on tables, and the bodies clambering up on to podiums to let the world see how young and beautiful they were in the young summer. It seemed that the gangsters meant no harm, and that Masha might have meant it when she kissed me. The pyramid looked like a pyramid, the fantasy smelled like happiness and the night felt like freedom.

* * *

We'd only been in bed for an hour or so when the light sailed over the water, through the trees and between our hotel curtains. I looked for signs and clues and stretch marks on Masha's hips and sleeping belly, but I couldn't find them.

FIFTEEN

It was full-on summer when we got back from Odessa. Spring happens in a hurry in Moscow, seeming to pass almost overnight or while you're watching a film: you wake up, or blink out of the cinema into the warming air, to discover it's been and gone. I could taste the hormones and the energy. Something had to happen with that energy, someone had to do something with it.

A few days after we flew home – a day or two before the date we'd fixed to sign the contract for the flats – Masha and I went to see Tatiana Vladimirovna again. She met us at the door, shooed us out, and together we went for a walk on the path around the thawed pond. We gave her another little present that we'd bought for her, a fridge magnet that depicted the

Odessa opera house and beside it the proud head of a tsarina. She held it up close to her eyes, then put it in the inside pocket of her skimpy navy spring coat. She said she'd love to go to the Black Sea again one day.

'You will,' I said.

'Maybe,' she said.

After that Masha told her that there was a problem with the apartments. In fact there were two of them. The first problem, which according to Masha I had identified, was that if Tatiana Vladimirovna swapped her apartment for the new one as they'd agreed, she might have to pay hundreds of thousands of roubles in property tax. The authorities, Masha said, would calculate what they thought the new place was worth, and add that figure to the fifty thousand dollars to determine the nominal value of her old home. The total would be above the threshold at which property tax kicked in. So Tatiana Vladimirovna might lose the fifty thousand and maybe have to pay more besides.

'Is this correct, Nikolai?' Tatiana Vladimirovna asked me. I don't know why she trusted me so much. Masha was looking me in the eye, not winking or encouraging or slyly nodding, just knowing what by then I was ready to say and do.

'It's true,' I said, in my best lawyer's voice, even though this was the first I'd heard of it. I checked later: it wasn't. But it sounded true.

There was a solution, Masha explained. They could make two separate contracts: one for the sale of Tatiana Vladimirovna's flat by the pond, just for the fifty thousand dollars, then another one for the purchase of the new place in Butovo. On the second contract they would set some fair-sounding price for the Butovo purchase, a number high enough so the authorities wouldn't think the sale was a sham. But the figure wouldn't be important because Tatiana Vladimirovna wouldn't actually have to pay it.

'Two contracts,' said Tatiana Vladimirovna. 'I see. How long until we sign the second contract, the one for my new home?'

'It will be soon,' said Masha. 'Very soon.'

Tatiana Vladimirovna stopped walking and looked down towards her shoes for a second. She shrugged and said, 'Okay.'

The second problem, Masha said, was that Stepan Mikhailovich had called to say the apartment in Butovo was almost ready, but not quite. It would be ready in a week or two, he promised, three weeks at the very most. But Masha suggested that Tatiana Vladimirovna should go ahead with the sale of her place anyway – she should sign the papers, take the money. She said we'd already made an appointment at the bank where the cash would be counted, and we would have to pay for it now even if we postponed the deal. (In those days, property sales, like all major Russian transactions – buying off judges, bribing tax inspectors – were always and only done in cash.)

'For that we have to pay?'

'Yes, Tatiana Vladimirovna,' I said.

However, Masha went on, Tatiana Vladimirovna would be able go on living in the place by the pond until Butovo was finished. It was just the kitchen to go, she said, Stepan Mikhailovich was putting in the worktops and the dishwasher and then it would be done. The only thing Tatiana Vladimirovna would have to do was de-register from her old building – that is, tell the authorities that she was no longer living there. She would be living nowhere. Masha said all this with no hurry or stumbling, no obvious nerves or emotion. She was amazing.

'Dishwasher!' said Tatiana Vladimirovna, and she laughed. Then she paused, a long pause during which I worried that she would consent but – I admit – worried more that she wouldn't. I remember looking down at the ground and thinking how miraculously dry the path around the pond was. The trees looked alive again, almost pure green, and there was a banging coming from the restaurant tent on the other side of the water. The magical animals crawling and pouncing on the wall of the building opposite Tatiana Vladimirovna's shone as though they'd been groomed for the summer.

Finally Tatiana Vladimirovna said, 'Okay. Let's meet at the bank,' and the three of us walked on.

* * *

The buried Zhiguli had emerged from its cocoon of snow in my street. It had a crack in the windscreen but looked cleaner than it did before it disappeared, as if its stains had been washed away by the winter. When I passed the building where Oleg Nikolaevich's friend lived, or used to live, I saw that a team of Tajik workmen were shlepping wheelbarrows of sand, bundles of plywood and vats of paint up the stairs. The summer café on the corner of the Bulvar had thrown open its shutters to let in the caressing air. The poplar trees that some genius Soviet planner had planted all over the city were on heat, sending out their furry white seeds – a benign June plague Muscovites call 'summer snow', which sticks in your hair and sometimes your throat, and collects along the gutters in clumps that drunk adolescents set fire to.

The bank we used for signing the final contract and counting the cash was close to Tatiana Vladimirovna's apartment, in the part of Moscow known as Kitai Gorod, China Town. There was a gambling hall next door, I remember, and a discount DVD store opposite. I was late. It was during the week, a Monday I think, and we were busy in the office with another new loan. The cash was still cascading in to Moscow, even after what the Kremlin had done to that uppity oil tycoon, his unfortunate lawyer and his livid minority shareholders. When I arrived they were huddled on the pavement outside the bank, Masha and Katya both in trouser suits that I hadn't seen before (tight at the hips), Stepan Mikhailovich with his rat-tail and a vaguely tweed jacket, Tatiana Vladimirovna in a long pleated skirt and brown blouse. We went inside, past a line of moody tellers behind their fortified windows, through a security-coded door and into a sort of boardroom, its windows high up near the ceiling like in a prison, tepid water in a decanter on the table.

There were two bank officials waiting for us: one to counter-sign the documents to be sent to the state property registration bureau, the other to count the money, which Stepan Mikhailovich had brought with him in a fraying leather briefcase. (I never did know where the other twenty-five thousand dollars came from.) In the far corner of the room there was a doorway, and across it they had one of those sliding metal security grates that you see outside shops when they've locked up for the night. They opened the gate, and we processed through the door in single file and down a metal spiral staircase – the bank people, Stepan Mikhailovich, Tatiana Vladimirovna, and me as her legal representative – silent apart from our footsteps and a couple of gasps from the old lady. She was in front of me, and when someone locked the gate behind us, screeching it across the threshold and then bolting it, I saw her head half turn back in some automatic Soviet spasm.

The room at the bottom was a windowless, airless, merciless vault, with a small wooden table in the middle, the kind you and I took exams on in the old days, and a solitary light dangling above it. The walls were made of safety deposit boxes. The woman from the bank whose job it was to count the cash – plump, middle-aged, Armenian I think, friendly in an exhausted sort of way – sat down in the only chair. Stepan Mikhailovich took the money, fifty thousand dollars worth of thousand-rouble notes, out of the briefcase and handed it to her to scrutinize. The rest of us stood around her, breathing, while she fanned out the notes under a fluorescent lamp. She looked at them through an eyepiece like the ones diamond dealers use, then ran the money in stacks through a noisy counting machine. She divided the bills into three piles, strangled them with elastic bands and put them inside a charcoal-grey deposit box. She made out a form, and finally slid the deposit box into a slot in the wall.

We panted up the stairs. Tatiana Vladimirovna sat down at the table with Stepan Mikhailovich. I stood against the wall between Masha and Katya. Tatiana Vladimirovna signed the new sales agreement that I'd got Olga the Tatar to draw up for us in a hurry: just her flat for our fifty thousand dollars. She signed quickly, without reading the document, and turned towards us to smile. A copy of the agreement would be sent to the property registration bureau, the bank people explained. When, in a week or two, they estimated, the bureau sent back the certificate declaring Stepan Mikhailovich was now the owner, he would get the duplicate set of keys to the property that the bank would be holding, and Tatiana Vladimirovna could come back for the money.

'Congratulations!' said Masha.

'Oi, Tatiana Vladimirovna!' said Katya, and lunged forward to hug her from behind as she sat at the table.

'Congratulations!' I said.

'Thanks,' said Stepan Mikhailovich.

'Dishwasher!' said Tatiana Vladimirovna, and laughed.

* * *

Vyacheslav Alexandrovich the surveyor went missing again around that time. The loan had been disbursed in full, but he was supposed to confirm that all the terms and deadlines were being observed – in particular that the terminal would deliver its first oil that summer, and thus that the project company was on course to meet the repayment schedule. But his phone was switched off, and he'd set up a mysterious auto-reply message on his email account that said he was extremely sorry, please forgive him, it might be some time before he was able to respond. The Cossack was all of a sudden incommunicado too. Sergei Borisovich went round to the building opposite the Kremlin where we'd had our last meeting with him. It turned out to belong to an oil-trading firm owned by an obese Uzbek murderer. They told Sergei Borisovich they'd never heard of the Cossack and escorted him out of the building. When we contacted Narodneft they reminded us, in writing, that they had no legal responsibility for any undertaking made by the joint venture. Paolo said there was no reason to trouble the banks yet, but I could see that he was stressed: he had dark circles under his eyes and he'd started swearing in Italian. He kept referring to the Cossack as 'the friend of Nicholas'. People avoided him in the office, and jumpily watched the red numbers tick up above the door of the lift, willing theirs to arrive, if they got stuck inside it with him.

I couldn't get away from work the day the certificate came through, so I wasn't there to see Tatiana Vladimirovna waddling off, as I imagined her doing, with fifty thousand dollars worth of roubles in a plastic shopping bag, heading back to the flat she'd lived in for forty years and expected to stay in for a few more weeks. It definitely would have happened, though, about ten days later, around the middle of June, when the days are longest and the winter seems like a dream. They couldn't fix that part. The bank was in charge, and the people there would only have given the money to her. So she must have had it, at least to begin with.

But before I left her, on the day they counted the notes down in the vault, Tatiana Vladimirovna invited us up to hers for the last time. It was only a short walk from the bank. Her boxes were dutifully stacked in the corridor. The furniture looked naked and embarrassed. The plates and certificates had been taken down from the wall. There was a bunch of flowers in the kitchen sink, which Tatiana Vladimirovna said her colleagues at the museum had given her, along with a new radio, when she'd left her job at the end of the previous week.

She gave me a present too. She said she had too many things, she didn't know whether she had room for all of them in Butovo, what use did she have for such things? She wanted me to have a memento of our friendship. It was the photo of her inside the gymnastic wheel, taken when she still had four decades of communist lies and shortages ahead of her, before a decade of hope, more lies and shortages, and finally Masha, Katya and me. I tried not to take it, but she insisted. I think you saw it once in a drawer, and asked me who it was, and I mumbled something about souvenirs but didn't really answer. Of everything I own – not all that much, admittedly, for a man of my age and bank balance – that photo of Tatiana Vladimirovna in her black and white youth is the thing I would be most happy to lose, the possession I would most like to escape from, but somehow can't.

SIXTEEN

Like I said, it was the smell.

The flowers were back in their beds in the middle of the Bulvar, gaudy regiments of pansies and tulips. In accordance with a secret clause in the Russian constitution, half the women under forty had started dressing like prostitutes. The warmth and the petrol fumes were creating a hazy mirage effect above the casinos on the Novy Arbat, as you looked up towards the river and the Hotel Ukraina. It was the middle of June, and Konstantin Andreyevich started to smell.

I was leaving my apartment in the early evening, on my way, I remember, to meet Steve Walsh at the American diner up near Mayakovskaya Square. When I walked down the stairs to Oleg Nikolaevich's landing I found George sitting on the mat outside their front door. He was an old, arthritic white cat, with pink ears and disconcertingly pink eyes, fat like he was pregnant but with a bone-skinny tail. He was staring at the wall as if he was suffering from post-traumatic stress. I leaned over him and rang Oleg Nikolaevich's bell, more than once, but there was no reply. George's empty pink eyes and my eyes met. I left him there and headed down the stairs to the front door and the tasty evening air.

I saw Oleg Nikolaevich first. He was facing away from me but I could tell it was him, standing there in a crumpled suit, his head down like he was praying or weeping. There were other people moving and talking all around him, but he was standing perfectly still and alone, and nobody was talking to him.

From the way I came, the crowd was blocking my view. But I caught the smell immediately – the rotting-fruit smell that had given Konstantin Andreyevich away. From about ten metres away, I saw the foot.

There was only one, stepping out of the boot of the orange Zhiguli, hanging down over the smudged number plate. The foot still had its shoe on, I remember. Above the shoe there was a stretch of sock, and above the sock there was a glimpse of greenish flesh.

From the knee up he was still in the boot and out of sight,

thank Christ, but somehow I knew straight away that it was Konstantin Andreyevich, Oleg Nikolaevich's missing friend. I reached Oleg Nikolaevich and stood alongside him, saw the thinning white swirls on the top of his bowed head, and looked at the ground with him for three minutes or a century, me and him, apart and together. Oleg Nikolaevich hadn't glanced up or sideways but I knew he knew I was there.

Finally I said, 'Terrible. Just terrible.'

He looked up and at me, opened his mouth, swallowed and looked down again.

There were five or six policemen standing around the car. Two or three of them were talking on mobile phones. They were wearing those funny blue shirts – stretched over the belly and elasticated around the waist, the gun slapping against the thigh below – that the Moscow police go in for in the summer. They looked like guests at a slow Russian barbecue. On the other side of the car, sitting on the bonnet and smoking, was the teenage detective who I'd gone to see and refused to bribe a few months before, when I'd been trying, albeit not very hard, to help Oleg Nikolaevich find his doomed friend.

'Hi,' I said.

'Hi, Englishman,' he said. He seemed pleased to see me. He was wearing black jeans, a linen jacket and a dark T-shirt with a picture of a pint of Guinness on the front.

'Do you know who did it?' I asked him.

He laughed. His acne had got worse. 'Not yet. Maybe tomorrow.'

'Why did they leave the body here?'

'I don't know,' the detective said. 'Probably they were moving it, and someone disturbed them. Probably they decided it was too dangerous to drive around with the old man in the boot. Maybe they meant to come back later but never got round to it. It looks like he's been in there a while. Maybe since last year.'

I remembered what Steve Walsh had told me about the amateur hitman/professional hitman murder method. I asked the detective whether that might have been how it went with Konstantin Andreyevich.

He thought for a few seconds. 'Could be something like that,' he said. 'It was a lousy job. Hammer, I think, or maybe a brick. Do you want to see?'

'No thanks.'

I walked a little way off, up to the churchyard fence. Yellow grass was trying to make a life for itself in the mud. I called Steve.

'He's dead,' I said.

'Are you going to be late? I thought we'd go to Alfie's Boarhouse afterwards.' Alfie's was a dive near the zoo where Russian girls pretending to be hookers, and hookers pretending not to be, went to dance on the tables and be ogled by middle-aged expats. I'd always liked Alfie's.

'Konstantin Andreyevich,' I said, 'my neighbour's friend. He's dead.'

I told Steve about the foot and the hammer (or brick).

'Told you he was dead,' Steve said. And then he said, 'It was probably for his apartment.'

'What?'

'His apartment. Does he own an apartment?'

'Yes,' I said. 'He does. He did.'

'So,' Steve said, 'that's it. That's the story, I'm telling you. It's always for the apartment, except when it's drink or adultery. Someone whacked him for his apartment.'

Property crime had been even more brutal in the nineties, Steve explained, with the tone of nostalgia Moscow veterans always adopt to talk about that cherished decade of larceny and lust. After communism, the Moscow government gave away most of the flats in the city to whoever was living in them for next to nothing. The scams started immediately, Steve said. Sometimes the crooks married the owners, then brought their cousins or brothers up from Rostov or wherever to get rid of them so they could inherit. Or they just tortured the poor fucks into signing over their titles, then dissolved them in acid or dropped them into the Moscow River.

'But now that Russia's gone civilized,' Steve said, 'they've worked out a cleaner way. They find some lonely old-timer, whack him, and get a bent judge to certify that they're the dead guy's lawful heirs. That's it, the place is theirs.'

'Don't they need a body?' I said. 'I mean to prove he's dead. Wouldn't they need him to be found?'

'Jesus, Nick, I thought you were the lawyer. No, no body necessary. In Russia, after you're gone for five years, you're dead. *Finito*. But – and this is the beautiful part – a friendly court can pronounce someone dead six months after he disappears. The claimant just has to show that the missing person was last seen in a dangerous situation. Which isn't difficult. Could be ice fishing. Could be swimming in the river while drunk. Could be picking the wrong mushrooms in the forest. Six months, he's dead and the apartment's theirs. When did Konstantin Whateverovich get lost?'

'I don't know,' I said. 'I can't remember. October maybe. Something like that.'

'Long enough. And long enough for them to sell it on.'

Up till that moment I think I'd managed to tell myself, to the extent that I really thought about it at all, that it wasn't so terrible, the thing with Masha and Katya and Tatiana Vladimirovna – that it might not be nice, might even be bad, but it wouldn't be *that* bad. Not like this. I should have listened. I could have guessed. Perhaps I did guess and carried on as if I hadn't. But when Konstantin Andreyevich stepped out of the boot of the Zhiguli, and Steve gave me his brief history of apartment fraud, I couldn't pretend not to understand any more.

'But to arrange the judge,' I said, 'the con men would need money, right? They'd need friends. What if you don't have them? I mean the criminals. What if they're small-time, they're from out of town, just a couple of youngsters?'

'There are other methods,' Steve said. 'You need a dupe, preferably with no relatives. You need a bit of patience and ingenuity, I suppose, but you can still do it. It happens all kinds of ways. It's the perfect Moscow crime. Privatization plus rocketing property prices plus no scruples equals murder. Anyway, what makes you think they're small-time?'

'I don't,' I said, backtracking. 'I don't know.' After a few seconds I said, 'He was in a car, Steve. In my street. In the snow. I mean, the car was in the snow. It looks like he was there all winter. He was buried in the snow.'

'Snowdrop,' said Steve. 'Your friend is a snowdrop.'

That's what they call them, he told me – that's what they call the bodies that come to light with the thaw. Drunks mostly, and homeless people who give up and lie down in the snow, and the odd vanished murder victim. Snowdrops.

'Like I told you, Nicky,' Steve said, 'when the end of the world comes, it will come from Russia. Listen, you coming to Alfie's?'

I hung up and walked back over to Oleg Nikolaevich. He'd straightened up but he hadn't moved.

'Oleg Nikolaevich,' I said, 'I'm very sorry. I'm very very sorry.'

'God is in his heaven,' said Oleg Nikolaevich, looking at the foot, 'and the tsar is far away.'

* * *

I could say it was my conscience that made me do it. I'd like to tell you it was my conscience. Maybe it even was conscience, as well as curiosity, and also something else, something uglier, a sort of awe at what I'd been part of that was a distant relative of pride. I'd also like to be able to say that I did it immediately, that it was the same evening, the night of the foot. But the truth is that it wasn't that night, or maybe even the next day. It was soon though, I'm sure it was soon, within a week, maybe only a week, that I went to look for Tatiana Vladimirovna. Even though I wasn't at all sure I'd find her.

I hadn't spoken to Masha or Katya since the day we'd all gone to the bank for the money counting and the signing. That was something I wasn't expecting – the suddenness of the end.

I'd called Masha's number over and over, but I only got the Russian out-of-order signal – three sharp notes, starting at a pitch high enough to shatter glass or derange dogs, then getting higher – and a demoralizing network message that said her phone was switched off or out of coverage. I tried again when I started to think about the old woman. In the end I went round to Tatiana Vladimirovna's and buzzed.

I buzzed for a minute, maybe two, standing in the shadows of her courtyard on a lovely warm Saturday. Finally a Japanese woman opened the door from the inside, I smiled at her and went in and up the stairs. I knocked on Tatiana Vladimirovna's front door, quietly at first, like there might be a baby inside sleeping, or as if I didn't really want whoever was there to answer. Then I knocked louder and louder, faster and faster, like I was the KGB on a busy night. But no one came, except a fat blonde woman in a dressing gown and hair curlers who rolled halfway down the stairs from the floor above, clung to the banister and stared at me until I left.

Outside I stood on the path around the pond. By then it was parched and dusty, an off-white dust that rose in puffs, blurring my trousers and tasting of chalk. I walked up to the Metro and through the glass swing doors, the heavy doors that lash back at passengers like their history. I'd given up holding them open, as I once had, for whoever came after me, instead letting them go without looking, turning down that free chance to show some mercy in that gladiatorial city.

I rode the Metro out to Butovo: in theory there might have been time for Tatiana Vladimirovna to have moved there. This time the taxi driver I flagged down outside the station was a breezily aggrieved Uzbek, who explained to me that soon, any minute now, the Muslims would rise up against the Russians and the rest for the final war. When we turned the corner at the edge of the city I saw that the other side of the road had become a jungle, the trees and bushes erupting with their Russian summertime urgency. I could see people trickling into the forest between the old wooden houses, carrying babies and bottles. We pulled up outside the building on Kazanskaya – Tatiana Vladimirovna's building, or Stepan Mikhailovich's, or MosStroiInvest's, or nobody's.

I buzzed the number of the flat we'd been to during the winter on the intercom panel. No one answered. I pushed all the numbers together and in random combinations. This time that trick didn't work. After a while I realized that the wires coming out of the intercom, one green, one red and one blue, were dangling unconnected beneath it. I banged my fist on the metal door. I crossed the road and looked up at the building.

The sun was behind it and I had to squint. As far as I could see there were no lights on anywhere inside. I stared for a long time at the corner window behind the balcony on the seventh floor that was supposed to belong to Tatiana Vladimirovna. Nothing seemed to be alive behind it. I thought I could just make out the kitchen cupboards on the back wall, but nothing else. The balcony was bare. Then I looked further up and saw that on the top floor the windows hadn't been fitted yet. One of those fat Moscow crows was perched on a gaping sill in the middle of the penthouse.

I started to walk back in the direction of the Metro station. I decided – what could it cost me? – to ask somebody about the building. I knew I wouldn't ever be in Butovo again. I marched through the overgrown grass in the yard of the nearest dacha and up to the front door. I didn't see the gigantic brown dog asleep next to a woodpile until afterwards. I knocked. An oldish man came to the door – he was maybe seventy-five, maybe fifty, it was always hard to tell. He was wearing a winter coat but no shoes or socks on his feet.

I apologized for the intrusion and asked whether he could tell me anything about the new building over the road.

'No,' he said.

'Nothing?'

He studied me for a few seconds, I guess deciding what kind of con-man I was. He had blood-flooded eyes, three days worth of pale stubble and intermittent teeth.

'I think,' he said, 'that they ran out of money.'

'Who ran out of money?'

'I don't know,' he shrugged. 'The bosses. They say they are going to knock it down.'

'Who say?'

'People.'

'Does that mean that nobody lives there?'

'Nobody,' he said. 'I mean, I don't know. The less you know, the better you sleep.' He offered me a jagged consolatory smile as he closed the door.

* * *

I had only a vague idea of where Masha and Katya lived, but I went to all the other places I could think of, or almost all. If you'd asked me then, I'd probably have said that I was still looking for Tatiana Vladimirovna, but that was only part of it, and not the main part, truth be told. There was my money, the twenty-five thousand dollars, but that wasn't really it either.

First I went to the mobile phone shop down by the Tretyakov Gallery. It was a hot day, and the shop was full of overheated customers fanning themselves with special-offer leaflets. The first girl I spoke to told me that Masha had quit and that she was busy. The manager said no, they didn't have any contact details for Masha, and asked me to leave. I went to the restaurant on Neglinnaya where I'd found Katya waitressing on New Year's Eve. They had a lot of Katyas, they joked, I could take my pick, but the one I was looking for was gone.

After Odessa I was pretty sure that Katya had never set foot in Moscow State University in her life. But I went up there anyway, to the manic Stalinist tower up on Sparrow Hills. I remember there was a young couple having their wedding photo taken on the esplanade that runs in front of the university and overlooks the city, above the river and the Kremlin, the churches and the chaos. The bride was in a strappy meringue dress, much less demure than I expect yours will be, if we're still on after this. Her friends were as colourful as peacocks, the first-boyfriend groom and the other men were in dour gangster suits. They looked touchingly doomed. I heard the guests shouting, '*Gorka, gorka*' (bitter, bitter), the ritual cue for the couple to embrace, and so kiss away all bitterness and make their new life sweet. The statues on the university's façade, of heroic intellectuals wielding books, patting globes and staring idiotically into the future, reminded me of the ones on the platform at Ploshchad Revolyutsii station, the platform where I'd first seen Masha. The security guard at the main entrance wouldn't let me in to the green entrance hall, though I'm not sure what I would have done in there even if he had. I stood outside, asking pretty girls in short skirts and boys in cheap jeans if they knew Katya, until I felt ridiculous and humiliatingly old. A rollerblader almost knocked me over as I was leaving. The star on top of the main spire winked in the fierce sunshine.

I phoned MosStroiInvest. It took a while – I think they were going bust – but eventually I got through. They said they'd never heard of Stepan Mikhailovich or Tatiana Vladimirovna. I figured Stepan Mikhailovich must have had a friend inside the company or among the contractors, someone who could have lent him the keys for Butovo. Maybe the idea started with that, with the bait. They must have had another friend or two who sorted out the phoney documents. That would have been almost all it took, plus me to put together the real ones for Tatiana Vladimirovna's apartment and keep her happy. They must have thought that giving her the fifty thousand helped to make the whole thing look genuine.

The only place I suppose I could have gone and didn't was the dacha, the one they said belonged to the old man who used to work for the railway – the one with the wardrobe-sized *banya* and the magical bedroom in the eaves, the place where I found out that Masha and Katya weren't sisters. Somehow it just felt too holy, a memory I wanted to freeze in the winter ice, and not tarnish in the sweat and let-down of the summer. It just seemed too much. You might think I could have gone to the police, that I should have gone to the police. I can see you thinking that. But what would I have told them? What had happened? A woman had sold an apartment. Some girls had gone away. Nothing had happened. And anyway, whatever had been done, I had done it too.

There was one time, in those few days when I was looking, when for a minute I thought I'd seen Tatiana Vladimirovna, or maybe I just let or made myself think so. It was on Tverskaya, at the bottom near Red Square. I was walking up to meet Paolo for a nervous lunch at the summer café on the terrace outside the Conservatory. I thought I recognized her shot-putter form, her relentless gait – slow but determined like an advancing army – and her give-a-shit bowl haircut, about fifty metres ahead of me on the pavement. I stopped dead, just for a second, then ran. But the pavement was crowded, and there was a dense mob of tourists around a stall selling Lenin T-shirts and Stalin dolls. It was like in a dream when you run and run but somehow don't seem to move. By the time I got to the corner where the Central Telegraph building is, I'd lost her. I looked over the edge of the half-wall at the top of the steps down into the underpass. I swerved up Tverskaya as far as the Levis shop. The old woman had gone.

It's possible that it was her – I'm not saying that it wasn't. It could have been her. Possibly she's wandering around Moscow or St Petersburg right now, with fifty thousand dollars in a plastic bag and that baby smile on her face. Maybe they left it at that. After all, they had her flat and she would never have been able to get it back. The paperwork was all in order, thanks to Olga. There was nothing old Tatiana Vladimirovna could do about it and no one to complain to. Except me, maybe. She would've known where to find me if she'd been looking.

But she never came, and I doubt they would have wanted to see her standing on the pavement making a fuss, or just spending the extra money that could have been theirs. 'No person, no problem,' an old Russian saying went, and I suspect they would have fixed it so there wouldn't be any problems. It wouldn't have been difficult, even without the snow. I'll never know for certain, but that's what I think.

I'm not even sure that Tatiana Vladimirovna herself ever expected to move to Butovo, not really. Perhaps she didn't really think she'd ever get to pick mushrooms in the forest, swim in the pond, run her dishwasher and gaze at the cupolas of the church from her new balcony. I'm not certain what she expected, but I've started to think that all along everyone knew more than me, Tatiana Vladimirovna as well as Masha and Katya. That they kept it from me like you keep a dirty secret from a child, until you can't cover it up any longer. I sometimes think that in a bizarre way it might, all along, have been a conspiracy against me.

Or maybe not. Maybe instead – probably instead, being as honest as I can be – it was a conspiracy of me against me, to keep the truth from myself. The truth being that I'd crossed a line somewhere, at some moment in a restaurant, in the back of a cab, under or on top of Masha or in the lift at Paveletskaya Square. I'd somehow become the sort of person who would go along with it, whatever it was, sensing but not caring that it was no good, fixing the forms and smiling so long as I got what I needed. The kind of person I never knew I could be until I came to Russia. But I could be, and I was.

That's what I learned when my last Russian winter thawed. The lesson wasn't about Russia. It never is, I don't think, when a relationship ends. It isn't your lover that you learn about. You learn about yourself.

I was the man on the other side of the door. My snowdrop was me.

SEVENTEEN

In the end, under pressure from the bankers and our London bosses, Paolo and I went up north to check on the Cossack's oil operation for ourselves. We flew up from the abattoir-like domestic terminal at Sheremetyevo airport, on a plane seemingly held together by Sellotape and hope. It was beautiful from above, the Arctic landscape: the pine forests were still dusted with diehard ice, little streams slalomed and frothed among the trees and the sea was dark and calm.

The nearest airport to the site of the terminal was at Murmansk, the city where Masha and Katya said they had grown up. I hadn't clocked the connection until we made the trip. Now, looking back, it feels sort of fitting and hurtful at once that I ended up there. At the time I was excited, even though it was too late and things had gone bad. I was excited to see the parks they might have sat in, the pavements they walked on, the views that wallpapered their lives. My grandfather had been there too, of course, when it was hell on earth. But I don't think I thought much about him. There was a big war memorial at the edge of town, but I didn't visit it. I didn't have time.

The Cossack's project company had an address that the hotel receptionist said was in an old Soviet housing estate. She said it was up near the Ferris wheel that rotated very slowly on a hill above the docks. We called the number we had for the office but nobody answered.

On the second day Paolo and I went by ourselves to the spot on the coast from which, according to Vyacheslav Alexandrovich, the oil would very soon be pumped out through a pipeline to the supertanker. The road stopped a few hundred metres from the shore. We got out of the taxi and walked along a rough path. It was hot and there were mosquitoes. We slung our suit jackets over our shoulders and swore. On a flat stretch by the sea there was a square pit, about the size of a squash court, muddy but dried up, like a kidnapper in a thriller might keep a woman captive in. But there were no pipes, no supertanker and no oil. There was nothing.

Paolo lit a cigarette and smoked it in one drag. We stood up there for about ten minutes, taking in the dimensions of our fuckedness, or that's how it felt to me. Then we went back to the hotel to get drunk.

We sat at the bar on the top floor, run by a Dagestani barman and a Korean madam. We drank for a long time and a lot. It was light around the clock up there in the summer, and through the window at three in the morning we could see cranes standing around the docks, silhouetted like paralysed insects against the sentimental pink clouds, with seagulls wheeling around them. It wasn't really our fault, we told each other. We'd done all the paperwork right. Maybe we'd given the Cossack a little more slack than he deserved. Perhaps my mind had sometimes wandered. But we weren't engineers or private investigators: we were only lawyers. Basically, we agreed, we'd just been unlucky to be exposed when the Kremlin changed the rules – when someone decided that actually running businesses and siphoning off their profits month by month was too much like hard work, and that it would be easier just to fleece the banks instead.

All the same, we knew this would stick to us for ever. No partnership for me, probably the boot for Paolo, no bonuses for either of us, and very likely no more Moscow. No more no limits.

'Fucking British Virgin Islands,' Paolo said. I could make out a birdshit-covered Lenin statue in the square beneath the hotel. 'Fucking Cossack. Fucking Russia.'

His pupils had shrunk to vicious black dots. Later on I wondered about Paolo – I wondered whether, just maybe, he had somehow been mixed up in it. I thought about how he had been with the Cossack, about the times he'd seemed to be angry and that meeting at Narodneft on New Year's Eve when we'd approved the loan, trying to remember any moments or tells I might have missed. But it didn't add up to much or enough.

We drank to us, and then to Moscow and the weasel President. Paolo took one of the Korean madam's plump associates back to his room for comfort. I lay on my bed, looking out into the milky Arctic air. I felt like crying but I didn't.

A few hours later – I'm not sure what time it was, I was still drunk, and down, and also on a strange sort of high at the same time, the high of nothing more to lose – I got up, went out and strolled in the direction of the cranes and the docks. I crossed over a railway line on a graffitied footbridge and landed on a cargo quay. I heard music, and saw a café open a little way along the water.

It had a tiled floor and a counter and one human being, a fat man in an apron with crowdedly tattooed hands.

'Good morning,' I said.

'I'm listening,' he said.

'Coffee, please.'

He put a teaspoon of Nescafé in a cup and gestured at an urn of hot water at the end of the counter. I mixed the coffee and sat down. The café smelled of oil. An antique fridge gave off an ominous hum.

I remembered what Masha had told me about her father. I said to the café owner, 'Is this the base for the nuclear ice-breakers?'

'No.'

'Where are they?'

'Round the bay. There is a separate military installation. It is secret.' They kept the submarines there too, he told me. It was where they'd towed the one that sank a few years before, to fish out the bodies of those poor swollen boys. I could see that he wanted to talk but needed to pretend that he didn't.

'Is that where the *Petrograd* docks?'

'Which?'

'The *Petrograd*. It's an ice-breaker.'

'No. There is no *Petrograd*.'

'Yes there is. I'm sure there is. I mean, I think there is...Or maybe there used to be but they took it out of service?'

'No,' said the fat man. 'There is no *Petrograd*. I worked on that base for twenty-five years. I was a mechanic. There is no *Petrograd*.'

I cupped my coffee. My hands shook. I remembered another thing Masha had told me about her childhood in Murmansk.

'Tell me,' I said. 'The wheel – the big wheel.' I gestured over my shoulder in the direction of the hill it stood on. 'In the eighties, was it expensive? I mean, was it too expensive for some children to ride?'

'It wasn't there in the eighties,' the fat man said. 'They put it up in 1990. It was the last thing the Soviet Union did for us. I remember because I got married that year. After we signed the register, we went on the new wheel.' He looked down at the floor for a second, maybe fondly, maybe ruefully, I couldn't tell. 'It cost twenty kopecks,' he said. 'But in the eighties it wasn't there.'

* * *

Narodneft denied all liability for the Cossack's scam. They'd only promised to pump the oil and pay the fees, they pointed out, after the terminal was built. Their listing on the stock exchange was postponed. The assorted government ministries we petitioned told us to fuck off, only less politely. We never heard from Vyacheslav Alexandrovich the surveyor. They must have turned him, probably that first time when he went missing, then came back to us with his bogus report. Maybe it was threats, maybe money, maybe women, probably all three. I can't blame him. From our firm's perspective the only consolation was that our Arctic debacle was swamped by the spate of even worse Russian news: the big expropriations up in Moscow, the tanks down in the Caucasus, the fear and grudges that erupted in the Kremlin, and seemed to spread across Red Square and the whole shabby, stunning Russian continent. We got a few paragraphs in the *Wall Street Journal* and the *Financial Times*, and an honourable mention in a feature Steve Walsh stitched together about naïve bankers in the Wild East.

Soon afterwards the Russians and Americans started squaring up again, the Kremlin postponed the elections, and most of the foreigners started heading for the airports anyway. But I think Paolo would have stayed on if the company hadn't cut him loose to help pacify the bankers. I heard he moved to Rio.

Instead of being fired I was called back to London to work on due diligence in the corporate division at head office, as you know: to sit in the basements of companies that are being bought or sold, vet files and never under any circumstances speak to clients, a bit like being put back on traffic after you've been a detective. Back to the thin life I have now. The old university friendships that are all duty and awkwardness, the job that is killing me. You.

I think I might just have quit the firm and clung on in

Moscow, possibly tried to get a job with some up-and-coming steel magnate or aluminium baron, if I'd still had Masha. I knew she didn't really love me – she didn't have to love me. I would have carried on, I think, seeing her twice a week, taking her home twice a week, knowing there was no other or better me I could be somewhere else, anchored to Moscow by the heavy inertia of approaching middle age. I don't think I'd have worried too much about how much of what she'd told me had been true, or even about what she'd done. I could have lived without Tatiana Vladimirovna. I might have managed to forget about her. So I think that Masha was better than me in the end. She had Seriozha, so she had a better excuse. And she at least acted like she'd done something wrong. I don't know who was in charge, but I hope she got a decent cut.

A couple of days before I left Russia, I went once again to Tatiana Vladimirovna's old place. It was the last time, and to be honest I think it was more out of nostalgia than anything more moral or noble. I punched random numbers into the keypad in the courtyard until someone buzzed me in. I climbed the stairs to her apartment. The door had been padded in maroon leather since the last time I saw it, and a creepy security camera had been installed above the top left-hand corner, which tracked me as I approached the threshold as if it was about to zap me with a laser. I rang the bell, listened to the footsteps, felt the eye peering at me through the peephole and heard three or four locks turning and a bolt being drawn.

He was wearing a silk kimono and a green face pack and at first I didn't recognize him.

I said, 'Excuse me…' trailing off as I tried to place him. I knew I'd met him before, but I couldn't remember where. Through work maybe, I thought, or at a party somewhere, maybe that one time I'd been for the drinks they threw at the British embassy to celebrate the Queen's birthday.

'Yes?'

'Excuse me…'

I could see boredom and mild anxiety competing on his forehead as we stood there, both of us waiting for me to finish my sentence. Then I got it. It was the Russian in the plush coat who'd been leaving Tatiana Vladimirovna's as I was arriving a few months before. His hair was still impeccable. I peered around his silk shoulders and saw that the Siberian chandelier was gone, and the walls of the corridor had been painted racing green. The eternal parquet was still there. I heard a tap running and a radio playing. I thought, *They sold it on before they even got it from her.*

'I wanted to ask you, do you know where the old lady is, the one who used to live here? Where is Tatiana Vladimirovna?'

'No,' he said. 'I don't know. I'm sorry.'

He smiled and slowly closed the door.

I went outside and stood beside the pond. I thought I'd try Masha's number one more time, for the last time. This time it rang and rang and rang but didn't cut into the automated out-of-order message. It rang and rang and rang, and then she answered.

'Allo?' – in that impatient, time-is-money way the Russians have.

It didn't sound like Masha, and it took me a few seconds to work it out. It was Katya.

'Allo?'

'Katya?'

She went quiet. A bottle smashed somewhere on the other side of the pond, somewhere near the basking fantasy animals. I guess there must have been some credit left on the SIM card that they didn't want to waste. I guess they reckoned that I and anybody else they'd been trying to lose and didn't want to speak to would have given up dialling that number, and that they could safely switch it back on.

'Katya, it's me, Kolya.'

She was quiet again. Then, 'Da, Kolya.'

'How are you?'

'Normal.'

'Can I speak to Masha?'

'No, Kolya. It is not possible. Masha has gone away.'

'To see Seriozha?' I said, in a voice that didn't sound like me. 'Has she gone to see Seriozha?'

'*Da*, Kolya. To Seriozha.'

I hadn't thought it through properly, what I wanted to say, what I wanted to get out of it. I could hear her almost hanging up.

I went back to the beginning. 'Why me, Katya? Why did you choose me?'

She paused, I suppose trying to figure out if it could cost her anything to tell me the truth. She must have decided that there was nothing I could do to them.

'You watch us too long, Kolya. In Metro. We see you are easy. We have other possibilities. But then we see that you are lawyer. This for us was very interesting, very useful. Also foreigner is good. But it could have been another person. We need only someone she may trust.'

'So that was all? For Masha I mean. That was all. Just useful.'

'Maybe not all, Kolya. Maybe not. I don't know. Please, Kolya.' She still sounded the same, half child, but very tired. 'It was business,' she said. 'Just business.'

'Why the money too?' I said. 'Why did you take my money?'

'Why not?'

I remember that I wasn't as furious as I wanted to be.

'When I saw you at the Uzbek restaurant – you know, during the winter – why didn't you want me to say anything to Masha?'

'I worry maybe she will be angry. She will think maybe you see everything is not true. For me it is not good when she is angry.'

'Are you really cousins, Katya? Tell me. Are you really from Murmansk? Who is Stepan Mikhailovich?'

'This is not important.'

There was only one thing left.

'Where is she?' I said. 'Where is Tatiana Vladimirovna?'

She hung up.

* * *

The afternoon before I left Russia, the last day of four and half years that feel like a whole life, I went down to Red Square. I made my way around the Bulvar, past the summer café and the beer tents to Pushkin Square. Then I walked down Tverskaya and through the underpass beneath the crazy six-lane highway at the bottom. A small crew of diehard communists with ragged hammer and sickle flags and wild eyebrows were holding a demonstration, trickling in from the direction of the Ferrari showroom and the statue of Marx. There were about three hundred riot police, most of them sitting in the funny rickety buses that they always roll up in, a few outside smoking and tapping their truncheons against their shields. The Lenin impressionist was having his photo taken with a cluster of Chinese businessmen.

I walked up through the gates. In front of me the make-believe domes of St Basil's soared above the cobbles. Far above the Aztec mausoleum the giant stars on the Kremlin towers glowed blood-red in the sun. It was high summer, but even then you could sense that the winter was recuperating somewhere across the Moscow River, getting ready for its comeback. You could feel the cold germinating in the warmth. I stood in the middle of the square, tasting the air and the city, until a policeman came over and moved me on.

You've wanted to know why I haven't talked to you about Russia. It's partly because it seems so long ago and far away, my old life without a seat-belt, too hard to explain to anyone else, too private. I guess maybe that's true of all our lives. Nobody can ever live yours except you, whether you live it in Chiswick or Gomorrah, and there is only a limited point in trying to revive it in words. And it's partly that, the way it ended, it seemed best to let it die. I didn't think I could tell you the whole story, until now, so I've just kept quiet.

But it hasn't only been that. Since I'm being honest, or trying to be, since I'm telling you almost everything, I should tell you the other reason, maybe the main reason. It's up to you what you do about it.

Of course when I think about it there is guilt, there is some guilt. But most of all there is loss. That is what really hurts. I miss the toasts and the snow. I miss the rush of neon on the Bulvar in the middle of the night. I miss Masha. I miss Moscow.